Here's what readers have to say about *56 Water Street*:

"I couldn't put down the book. It was really good and entertaining."—Owen Bolhuis

"*56 Water Street* is an amazing book. It pulls you in from the first word until the moment you close the book. It's funny, adventurous, and even frightening. I would recommend this book to all my friends! Two huge thumbs up!"—Cree Toner

"This book was very sad at some points, but I loved it. It could make you sad or happy. I have read lots of books, but this book was better because it had a lot of detail and different settings. I got really excited when they went into the house for the first time and when they saw the ghost in the yard. I hope the author writes another book."—Aiden Patterson

"I really liked *56 Water Street*. It's like being pulled into another world. There were some really sad parts in this story and some happy parts. I really like this book. You should make more of them."—Nicholas Strangway

"I was so captivated by the story and the characters."—Lorraine Tasker

"A *real* page turner for all ages."—Debbie Harris

56 WATER STREET

56 WATER STREET

A Novel

Melissa Strangway

iUniverse, Inc.
New York Lincoln Shanghai

56 Water Street

iUniverse books may be ordered through booksellers or by contacting:

iUniverse
2021 Pine Lake Road, Suite 100
Lincoln, NE 68512
www.iuniverse.com
1-800-Authors (1-800-288-4677)

Because of the dynamic nature of the Internet, any Web addresses or links contained in this book may have changed since publication and may no longer be valid.

This is a work of fiction. All of the characters, names, incidents, places, organizations, and dialogue in this novel are either the products of the author's imagination or are used fictitiously.

ISBN: 978-0-595-42429-0 (pbk)
ISBN: 978-0-595-86764-6 (ebk)

Printed in the United States of America

For my father.

Acknowledgments

There are many people I would like to thank. Without their support, you would not be reading this book.

First, I would like to thank my children, Nicholas and Chantel, who sat patiently listening to the umpteen million changes to the pages of this book.

To my mom and dad, for their unconditional love and belief in *56 Water Street*. Without them and their knowledge and sometimes brutal scrutiny of this story, I might not have continued this incredible journey.

To my father, who has spent many hours on my dream. Because of him, it has now materialized. Without him, I would have never succeeded.

To everyone at iUniverse. Their professionalism and patience made this an enjoyable experience.

To Lorraine, my dearest friend. Miles separate us, but our friendship has proven to be everlasting. You are more than a season or a reason. You are an important part of my life.

To Wendy, who was always ready to read another draft.

To Sheri, my partner in crime, the brain behind all wonderful and sometimes crazy ideas. I can't even imagine how I existed before we met. You have been my strength when I was weak; you encouraged me when I was ready to give up. You know all my darkest secrets, and you let me cry on your shoulder when life seemed too foreboding. Our friendship now journeys into a lifetime.

To all the pioneer readers of *56 Water Street*. Thank you for all your encouragement. Your ideas are wonderful, and I hope I will be able to incorporate them in my next book.

To my feline, Samsker, who enjoyed prancing across my keyboard, adding his own creative bits to this story. He was always annoyed that no one in the story has a cat.

Finally, but certainly never least or last, to my husband, Tim. You truly are the wind beneath my wings. You lifted me up and let me fly and then stood in my shadow to let me shine. You have loved me through good times and held my hand through bad times. You refused to give up on me when I had already given up on myself. You are my best friend.

To all of the above, I am deeply indebted.

Thank you,
Melissa

Chapter One

On. Off. On. Off. The lights in the kitchen flickered. On the opposite side of the street, Derek and Ravine stood still and stared, temporarily paralyzed by the lights in the old house.

If anyone else had been paying attention, they might have wondered what the kids were staring at. But no one noticed them.

Water Street was noisy and alive with the hustle and bustle of summer and the anticipation that school would finish in a few days. Soon, the streets would be filled with kids all day, not just in the evenings.

Off. On. Off. On.

Without a word between them, and without looking at each other, Derek and Ravine slowly began to cross the street. Their hearts were pounding loudly against their summer shirts as they reached the sidewalk in front of the old place.

A few droplets of sweat trickled down Derek's face. He looked at Ravine. If she was trembling, he couldn't tell. She seemed calm but intensely focused on where they were going. Her hands were shoved deep into the pockets of her shorts.

All around them, young girls were busy skipping rope and playing hop-scotch in driveways. Boys were playing catch on the front lawns, close to their houses but far enough away so they wouldn't break any windows. Kids of all ages were riding bicycles along the sidewalk, swerving up onto lawns or down into the road to avoid the grown-ups out for a pleasant evening stroll.

On. Off. On. Off.

Derek and Ravine stood at the edge of the unkempt lawn, watching the weeping willow sway as if beckoning them toward the house. Neither of them said anything about the tree waving wildly even though there seemed to be no wind. Derek looked behind him and noted the trees across the street were not moving. Then he glanced again at Ravine. Her hands were still shoved in her pockets and she looked even more focused, if that was possible.

The sounds of tag, hide-and-go-seek, street hockey, and kids shooting water pistols filled the air as they had most evenings since the weather turned warm.

Off. On. Off. On.

Derek and Ravine now stood in front of the living room window.

Other residents of Water Street didn't notice the flickering light. They didn't even glance in the direction of the house. Number 56 wasn't a house that got any attention these days.

The lights flickered off in the kitchen. And then back on again.

Derek and Ravine stood up tall on their toes, stretching to see over the sill and peering through the dusty window. Then, as the light flickered on again, a figure appeared suddenly, as if out of nowhere.

Instinctively, Derek and Ravine both trembled and stepped back, looking at one another with wide eyes. Turning their attention back to the flickering light, they saw the tall figure was now coming toward them. Their next move was an easy one.

Run.

With no hesitation, they ran as fast as their ten-year-old legs could carry them, down the ragged lawn of Number 56 and back to the safety of the sidewalk on their own side of the road.

Water Street was a well kept, well maintained, neatly manicured, and respectable place to raise a family. And even though some of the residents had heard there was a black period in the street's past, none of them knew anything about it. The rumour said it had all started about a hundred years ago. Or had it been further back? But no one knew what kind of trouble there had been. After all, a hundred years, or maybe longer, was enough to bury the memory of what had happened. If anything ever did.

Whatever trouble had happened, local residents figured it had been swept aside. If the street really held dark secrets, people didn't give it much thought.

"A fine, fine place, that Water Street," is what people would say if they drove through the neighbourhood. The residents considered it a nice place to live. Many people envied them.

When Ravine and Derek were finally a safe distance from the house, they bent over, trying to catch their breath.

"Who do you think was in there?" Ravine puffed, her eyes still wide.

Derek shook his head. His wavy blond hair was now stuck to his forehead, and sweat was trickling down the sides of his face.

He and Ravine had been best friends as long as he could remember. To him, she wasn't a girl; she was just another one of his buddies. But his best buddy.

Anyway, you couldn't really call Ravine a girl. She had shiny, shoulder-length brown hair and usually wore brown-rimmed glasses, which she swore she didn't need. She was almost always dressed in jeans and T-shirts, like all Derek's buddies, and she was the only kid he knew who could hit a baseball right out of the park. He had only seen her in a dress once, and he wondered if she only wore them when something bad happened. She didn't fuss over her hair like the other girls he knew. Heck, she even had more dirt under her fingernails than he did. Ravine was definitely the coolest girl he knew. In fact, she was the coolest person he knew. Period.

"I have no idea," he replied, after catching his breath. He checked his watch. "I'd better split. I was supposed to be home ten minutes ago, and if I don't want my mom screeching my name up and down Water Street for the whole world to hear, I should get going now."

Without looking back, Ravine and Derek walked away from the house that nobody talked about. The house that no one went near.

Neither of them asked the other why they had run because neither would ever have admitted to being scared just because there was someone in the house. Or something.

As they walked, Derek wondered what the big secret about this house was. Why didn't anyone ever talk about it? What was everybody trying to hide?

Chapter Two

Children flooded the sidewalks and the wide brick road, enjoying their final hours before bed.

Derek and Ravine melted into the nightly scene of Water Street as they headed to their homes. For now, the street was in full commotion, and they walked silently past the other kids.

They lived just two houses apart and, as they headed to their front doors, Ravine was thinking there was something mysterious about 56 Water Street. And she knew they were going to find out just what it was. Even though they had been curious about the old, abandoned house ever since they were little, tonight was the first time she and Derek had mustered up the courage to go near it. The house was spooky, and it had taken them a long time to decide to venture toward it.

As they got closer to their own places, Ravine glanced at Derek, still thinking about the flickering light, still thinking about the house. Derek looked calm, but she knew him well enough to be sure he was shaking inside. Like she was.

Ravine walked up her driveway. Her house wasn't one of the historical homes like Number 56, or even an old farm house. Ravine's house was less than twenty years old and looked like most of the others going up around the neighbourhood—two-storey and faced with white stucco. These fancy new residences were slowly replacing the old houses, like the one across the street, with modern sameness.

Ravine climbed the stairs beside the carport and opened the front door.

"Is that you, sweetheart?" her mother called from the living room.

Ravine sighed. Of course it was her; she was an only child now. That thought stopped her, and she hesitated before answering.

"Yes, it's me, Mom!" she called back, pushing aside unpleasant memories.

Taking off her shoes, Ravine couldn't stop thinking about what she and Derek had seen. There was no sense trying to convince herself that it was a trick of the setting sun, and she was sure they weren't imagining things. The lights had really gone on and off; that must mean someone was flicking the switch. The tall, dark figure, she guessed. Something eerie was going on in that house. Something wasn't quite right.

She walked into the living room and, just as she expected, her mother was reading a book, and her father was watching television. She plopped herself into a chair and stared at her parents. She hadn't seen them laugh for such a long time.

"So what did you do outside?" her mother asked, turning a page of the new novel Ravine had bought her last week. Her mother read all the time now. Before, she always seemed to be busy running around. Ravine couldn't remember exactly what her mother used to do to stay so busy, but it was always something. She wished her mother would be busy again; she was happier then.

"Just hung out with Derek," Ravine replied.

Suddenly, her father laughed at something on the television. Ravine and her mother looked at him with surprise.

"What's so funny, Robby?"

He grinned widely and shook his head, still chuckling to himself. These days, he was a pretty serious guy, and it was rare to see even a smile on his lips. A loud, boisterous laugh was quite unusual.

Without waiting for her father to answer, Ravine started to speak.

"Derek and I saw something really strange tonight, Mom," Ravine said, looking at both her parents. For a second, she hesitated. Maybe telling her parents about the house wasn't such a good idea after all. Maybe they would scold her and tell her to stay away from there. But it was too late; she had already started.

"And what was that, sweetheart?" her mom asked distractedly, turning another page.

Ravine faltered and finally said, "The lights kept turning on and off across the street."

"Maybe they have a burnt out light bulb."

Ravine was confused. "What do you mean by that? If it burned out, it wouldn't have come on. Besides, they've probably been burnt out for hundreds of years."

Her mother laid the book in her lap with a sigh. "Don't be silly. I'm sure the Morgans change their light bulbs more often than that," she said, laughing. The tone of her voice said she wanted to get back to her novel.

"No, not the Morgan house; I'm talking about 56 Water Street. The lights were flickering on and off. Don't you think that's a little unusual? No one's lived there, well, forever."

Her mom looked up now, and her eyes opened a little wider, the book still on her lap.

Her father also turned toward her, ignoring his television program. He had only been half-listening to Ravine and her mother, but when Ravine mentioned the address, the smile quickly disappeared from his face. He frowned at Ravine.

Neither parent spoke. They were unnaturally quiet, and if Ravine had thought that a light going off and on across the street was odd, the expressions on their faces were definitely odder.

"Well," she added, cautiously, "don't you think that's strange?"

Her parents were staring at her as if she had two heads, two noses, and an extra ear.

"Ravine, what are you talking about?" her dad asked, quietly. His eyebrows creased together, and his frown deepened.

Ravine sighed. What was wrong with them tonight? Were they thick? Deaf?

"The lights were flickering on and off in the house at Number 56. What do you make of that?" she repeated, showing her annoyance.

She wished she hadn't gotten into this conversation. She had their attention, but the looks on their faces worried her. Whatever was wrong with her parents concerned her more than the house at Number 56.

Her mother shook her head. "Ravine, there is no house. The house at Number 56 was torn down ages ago. Long before we moved here." She paused for a second before adding: "Long before you were born, sweetheart, maybe even before your father and me were born. From what I've heard, anyway."

Still shaking her head, Ravine's mother continued. "Sweetheart, we really have no idea what you are talking about."

Ravine looked at her mother, then her father. And back to her mother. They didn't look like they were joking, and it would have been unusual if they were. What did she mean that the house was torn down? How could her parents not see the house standing there? It was the largest house on the street, kind of hard to miss. What the heck were her parents talking about?

She heard these thoughts so clearly in her head that she hoped she hadn't said them out loud.

Something was going on; something wasn't right. Ravine shivered. Of course there was a house there; she could see it, and Derek could see it too. In fact, looking past her father and out the window behind the couch, she could see it right now. Large as could be. Right across the street, standing right where it always was. You'd have to be blind to not see it.

She looked at her father. He nodded.

"Your mother's right. There hasn't been a house there in a very, very long time. The neighbours don't talk about it much. In fact, I'm not sure even the people who have lived here longer than us remember exactly when it was destroyed, or what actually happened. It was such a long time ago." He paused. "Are you okay, Ravine?"

They were not joking, and Ravine could see that. She sat very still, worried. For a moment she was numb, unable to speak or think clearly. A chill ran through her. They were serious; they really couldn't see the house across the road. But there it was, even more plain than the nose on her face. The broken shutters; the crumbling porch; the torn, dirty curtains that only partly covered the windows. She could see it all. Of course the house existed.

But she looked back to her parents, who were both wearing concerned expressions. She knew that look.

"You're scaring me, sweetheart," her mother said.

Ravine's mind was swimming—a house that she and Derek could see right across the road, and her parents didn't even know it existed? She knew she needed to offer a quick explanation for this.

"Just kidding!" she squealed with as much enthusiasm as she could muster. She had been taken completely off guard by her parents. "Joked ya! Really got you good this time, huh?"

Her parents continued to stare at her and then they looked at each other. Finally, her mother sighed, and her father returned to watching television.

"It's been quite a while since I've heard one of your crazy jokes," Ravine's father said without looking away from the television. "I think you really frightened your mother. For a moment, even I thought you were serious. I honestly believed you thought there was a house across the street."

Flipping through the channels, he seemed content with Ravine's explanation. Putting down the remote, he stood and said he was going to make some coffee.

"Do you want one, Linda?"

Ravine watched her parents as her mother settled back in her seat with her book and her father headed to the kitchen. Relieved that she had escaped this mess, she wondered if life would ever get back to normal for them. She wondered what normal was. It had been so long—maybe normal just wasn't possible anymore.

Without their noticing, Ravine slipped out of the living room quietly and headed upstairs to her bedroom. She closed the door behind her and walked toward her window, pulling back the curtains.

There it was. Number 56 Water Street. The house loomed over all the others on the block. It seemed darker and gloomier than the rest of the street and, whether the sky was cloudy or sunny, the house always had its own shadow. As she watched the weeping willow in the front yard swaying gently, she noticed that the breeze didn't affect any other trees or flowers. A darkness fell over her, sending a chill up her spine. It made her shiver, and she turned away from the window, quickly shutting the curtains.

As she leaned against her pillow, she thought about phoning Derek. But it was close to ten and, although the school year was almost over, he'd probably be getting ready for bed. Even if he wasn't, his mom would lecture her about phoning so late. Better not, she thought.

She picked up the small photo in a wood frame from her night table and touched the smiling face with her fingertips, like she did every night. It seemed as if it were only yesterday that everything was okay. Normal.

Ravine whispered loving words to the image, like she did every night, and then set her back on the night table. Ravine got into her pajamas and crawled deep under her covers even though the room was quite warm. She shut her eyes and started to think about Number 56.

Just then, a sudden summer breeze swept through her window and into her room, giving her a brief flicker of terror. It passed quickly, and she shuddered, thinking she must be tired.

But why could she see the house when her parents couldn't? She let that thought fade in and out of her mind until she fell into a restless sleep.

Slowly, a figure came into focus and stared at Ravine. The figure didn't look solid, but wasn't transparent either. It was the image of a girl, soft and fuzzy around the edges. The girl gazed at the sleeping Ravine. The figure sat on the edge of the bed, knowing she needed Ravine. She would not let her go, and she let that thought enter Ravine's mind. It wasn't like a dream; more like someone was getting inside her head. Ravine couldn't hear or see the image because she was asleep, but she felt the presence.

The figure played around with the scenes in Ravine's head for a while until, flickering like a candle in a soft breeze, the girl faded completely, leaving Ravine alone in the dark room.

But the figure would be back.

Derek was still sitting at his computer when his mother called to him to turn it off. It was bedtime. If only he had a couple more minutes.

"Ten more minutes, Mom," he yelled back as he continued typing.

"It's bedtime," she repeated.

Derek figured he could keep this yelling match going for at least five minutes before she stormed into the room. Then he could complain for five minutes about the injustice of having to go to sleep way too early. And he could finish the research he was absorbed in while the argument was in progress.

"Awww come on, Mom. Just ten more minutes." He typed in "56 Water Street" and hit the enter key.

"Derek, now. I'm not kidding!" she yelled.

His eyes grew big as he read, "One million, five hundred forty-six thousand matches found." Geez, this was going to be harder than he thought. He could already hear his mother's footsteps coming up the stairs.

"Derek, I told you it's time for bed," she said, standing right beside his chair.

"But Mom, I'm trying to find some information on 56 Water Street."

He continued to type until he noticed that the only sound was the clicking of the keys. He looked up at his mother, who was staring at him. He recognized that look: concern.

"The house across the street," Derek began. "There's got to be some information online, but I'm having a hard time finding it."

His mother still said nothing, but her look did not change. Derek stopped typing.

"What house are you talking about?" she asked quietly.

Derek pointed behind him, over his left shoulder, as he stared at the computer screen. He could see Number 56 from his window.

"There is no house there, Derek," his mother said slowly.

Derek's fingers stopped completely. "Of course there is! It's the oldest and biggest and ugliest house on the block." Derek looked at his mother with worry. She never kidded around; she was way too serious.

"I have no idea what you're talking about." She walked over and felt his fore-head. "Are you okay, Derek?"

His mind was buzzing as he realized with a shock that his mother couldn't see the house. He knew she wasn't playing a trick on him; she could not see the house even though he was looking out the window, staring directly at it.

His whole body was drawn to Number 56, as though it had some power over him. But he pried his eyes away and looked back at his mother.

"I mean the one that used to be there," he stammered, clearing his throat, and trying to get out of this conversation.

He was frightened; he knew what he saw. Why didn't she see it, too? He didn't know what was wrong with her, but now he wished he'd just turned off the computer when she had told him to.

"I've heard it was really old when it was torn down," he lied. "A bunch of kids at school were talking about it, and I got curious. I thought maybe I could find something about it on the Internet."

"Oh, okay," his mother said, looking relieved. "But not tonight. It's too late. You can continue your research another time."

She started to walk away but turned around. "You might want to search under Rupert or Roberts. The family that lived there many years ago was named something like that. But continue your searching some other time. You have to get up in the morning; the school year isn't over yet."

She reminded him once again to shut off his lights. "Good night, Derek." She closed his door behind her and headed back downstairs.

Derek stood up, his knees weak at the idea that had just hit him. Were he and Ravine being haunted by an invisible house? Were he and Ravine the only people who could see the house? He realized he'd never heard anyone else speak about it. What could this mean? He wanted to call Ravine right now and talk, but it was too late. It would have to wait until morning.

He walked over to his window. The old weeping willow across the street was blowing in a gentle night breeze that didn't seem to affect anything else. Although it was dark, the outline of the house was still visible. "Or at least," he thought, "I can see it." A cold chill ran down his arm as he shut the curtain.

As he climbed into bed, he was sure he could hear the beating of his heart, and the steady rhythm soon carried him into a restless sleep.

Chapter Three

Derek and Ravine walked to school together every day unless one of them was sick or something. But today, neither of them spoke until they got to the edge of the playground. Once there, they looked at each other, and they both started talking at the same time.

"What did you say?" they both asked.

Ravine answered first. "Something totally weird is going on, Derek. My parents say there is no house across the street. They say it was torn down years ago. How come we can see it and they can't? Do you think there's something wrong with my mom and dad?"

"Well, if there's something wrong with your parents, then there's something wrong with my mom, too. She doesn't see it, either."

Derek and Ravine stared at each other. Maybe they were the ones who were crazy. Maybe they were the ones losing their minds.

But they didn't have time to think about it further. As they walked into the schoolyard, they were surrounded by their friends. The mystery would have to wait.

The big countdown was on. There were only four more days until summer vacation; that was the good thing about today. The bad thing was that Derek and Ravine couldn't discuss the invisible house with all their friends around. Somehow, they each knew instinctively that they had to talk about this themselves before saying anything to their friends.

For now, they would need to focus on the important things the end of the school year brought, like packing up lockers, cleaning out desks, checking the box full of mitts and hats lost over the winter.

But the really important thing was getting ready for the big end-of-term carnival on Friday. The excitement was even rubbing off on the teachers.

The weather had already turned warm and fine, but inside the school, it was sweltering. The building was only a few years old, but the school board had decided not to install air conditioning in order to save money. Some teachers held their classes outside, and others cut classes short because of the heat.

Besides, it was summer; it wasn't just the kids who were anxious for school to end. Unlike the students, the teachers still had to conduct themselves with a bit of dignity until the last bell on the last day. They had to pretend they wanted to be at school.

The bell rang, but no one raced to the line, not even the teachers. The end of classes was too near to work up much enthusiasm for the school bell. The teachers stood outside, casually finishing up conversations before herding in the kids. Finally, the kids dawdled into line, with a few teachers still a couple of reluctant steps behind.

Ravine sat in her seat directly behind Derek. Shortly after class started, he stretched his arms over his head, pretending to yawn, and dropped a piece of paper on Ravine's desk. Discretely, she placed her hand over it and slid it toward her just as Mrs. Tackle walked by. Ravine looked up at her and smiled.

Mrs. Tackle had no tolerance for notes being passed, and usually, if she caught a student with one, she would read it aloud in front of the class. She had embarrassed a few students this year by reading some pretty interesting notes out loud. Most kids only had to learn that lesson once; kids who hadn't been caught, though, still felt pretty brave and willing to risk it.

The most memorable note was a really long, mushy one that Annie wrote to Joannie about her crush on Sunil.

Ravine and Derek had never been caught, and they probably passed more notes than anyone. They always had a lot to say.

When Mrs. Tackle was a safe distance away, Ravine quietly unfolded the paper. "Let's find out at recess if anyone else sees 56. And we gotta be careful in case it's only us."

Ravine refolded the note and stuck it in her desk. Then, she kicked the bottom of Derek's chair twice to let him know she had read it and agreed.

Ravine pondered what Derek had written. How could they possibly find out about the house without making it look too obvious? As Mrs. Tackle continued to speak, Ravine tried to think of different ways to ask her friends about a house that didn't exist. Should she just come out and say that while she and Derek were looking through the dusty, broken windows of spooky old Number

56 last night, somebody was in there flicking the lights on and off? Or should she joke about her parents trying to make her believe the house wasn't there?

It didn't make any sense; and the more she thought about it, the more confused she became. Why couldn't her parents see what was right there? Or Derek's mom? Ravine had a strange feeling that she and Derek might be the only ones who could see 56 Water Street. If that was the case, she was worried about talking to her friends. They might think she and Derek were nuts.

Derek kept watching Mrs. Tackle. He usually followed her every move around the classroom. Right now, her lips were moving, so he was pretty sure she was talking. But he wasn't listening; he was too busy thinking about the house and what a creepy feeling it gave him. Just thinking about the figure in the kitchen gave him goose bumps.

"Derek, have you and Ravine decided on the activity you are going to set up for the carnival?" Mrs. Tackle asked.

No answer.

"Derek! I need to know what you two have decided."

The last week of school was always like that; the bodies might be here, but the minds were already off on vacation.

Mrs. Tackle tried again. "Paging Derek Radley!"

No answer.

Ravine kicked the bottom of his chair, jolting Derek back to reality at the same time she answered for him.

"Derek and I have decided to put together a fortune teller tent. I contacted Madame Jewels, and she said she would read fortunes. The school only has to pay her twenty-five dollars, so Derek and I figured if we charged two dollars a reading, we could cover the costs and make a profit for fundraising."

Mrs. Tackle nodded her head. "Sounds interesting, Ravine. Will she be here for the whole carnival?"

"Yeah, Mrs. Tackle. She will be," Derek said.

Mrs. Tackle turned to him and smiled. "It's very nice of you to join us after all, Derek."

The class laughed, and Derek looked down at his desk, blushing. As his face grew red, it made his hair look even blonder.

The bell rang just in time for him to avoid any further embarrassment. Without waiting to be dismissed, Derek ran for the door with the rest of the class, like the school was on fire.

Kids flooded onto the playground, and Ravine and Derek finally caught up to their friends.

As they approached, they heard Lisa saying, "My mom's making me take tennis lessons again this summer."

"What's the big deal? She makes you do that every summer. Why don't you just tell her you don't like tennis?" asked Sunil.

"I can't. She thinks it's a great sport. She's been playing it ever since she was, like, five or something. She'd be pretty mad if I told her I thought it was boring."

"Do you still have to go downtown to play?" asked Joannie.

"Yeah. My mom always says they should build some tennis courts in our neighbourhood."

"Yeah, but where?" asked Sunil.

"What about at 56 Water Street?"

Everyone turned to look at Derek and seemed stunned by his question. No one said anything right away, and it was Ravine who finally broke the silence.

"Why not?" she asked.

"Don't you know that lot is haunted?" Lisa asked. Her big brown eyes were open wide, looking at them in disbelief. Everyone else nodded.

"Haunted? How?" Derek asked.

"Are you kidding? Anyone who walks onto the lawn of Number 56 disappears and is never seen again," said Joannie. "How come you don't know that? You live right across the street from the place."

Ravine and Derek looked at each other. Then they looked at their friends and they both snorted.

"Don't be ridiculous," Ravine scoffed. "You don't expect us to believe this nonsense, do you?"

"It's true," Sunil said. "Lisa's right. The whole place just looks spooky. Man, where have you guys been the last ten years?"

The group laughed nervously and started to tell stories about the haunted property.

Sunil said his dad told him that a construction company had put a bid on the lot about forty years earlier. They were going to build an outdoor pool for the neighbourhood kids. But the day the workers arrived to start digging, everyone just disappeared. People saw the workers walking toward the property, but they couldn't say what happened after that. All anyone knew was that the workers were gone and never seen again. The big trucks and diggers and rollers and pavers sat on the road for months before city workers came and took them away.

After a while no one talked about it. Apparently everyone just figured there was some reasonable explanation, probably some kind of fight between the construction workers and their boss. Eventually the disappearance had been forgotten.

Until the Smith twins vanished five years later.

Rumours started to fly almost immediately. The boys were in their late teens, and it was possible that they just ran away because their father was not a nice man. Whatever the story was, it was enough to start people whispering about 56 Water Street again. Some said the property swallowed them up, just like it must have done to the construction workers. Most folks thought that kind of talk was crazy. But still …

Nothing ever linked their disappearance to the house, but that didn't stop people from believing the house at Number 56 had something to do with it. The twins never did show up, and no bodies were ever found. After many months of searching for them, the public forgot the mystery.

"Sunil's right," Joannie added. Then she told them the stories she had heard from her grandmother about how every *For Sale* sign that was placed on the property disappeared, and anyone who stepped on the lawn vanished into thin air. People stayed away from the property and pretended that it didn't exist. Eventually, they stopped talking about the disappearances. Joannie's grandmother even said that a priest had condemned the property, saying it was cursed.

Over the years, people in the area just blocked the property from their eyes and minds altogether.

"It's so cool. Like the Bermuda Triangle," Lisa said, "but right on Water Street."

"Man, it's like a black hole," Sunil agreed.

All the kids nodded and, one after another, they told the stories they had heard about ghosts and other strange things at Number 56.

But none of them had any idea how long ago the house had been torn down.

Ravine and Derek listened with quiet interest. At least they knew now that no one else could see the house. But since they could, there was still the possibility they were both crazy.

"This is stupid. You guys don't really believe all this, do you?" Derek asked, laughing at his friends.

"Yes, great campfire stories," Ravine added.

The bell rang.

"Well, it's true, dude," Sunil said to Derek as they walked toward the line. "I wouldn't go anywhere near there."

Joannie and Lisa nodded.

"Why do you think only you and I can see the house?" Ravine asked as she and Derek walked home from school. She swung her backpack onto her shoulders. It was getting heavier every day with all the junk she had to bring home for the summer.

Derek shook his head; it didn't make any sense. "We can both see the house, touch the house, even smell it. But everyone else says they don't see anything. And I don't think they're lying. I know I'm not crazy, and I'm pretty sure you aren't either. Although sometimes …"

Ravine adjusted her backpack to free her left hand, and she punched Derek in the arm. Hard.

"We need to find out if we disappear when we walk on the lawn of Number 56. I mean, if no one else can see the house, maybe they can't see us when we're standing beside it," Derek said, rubbing his arm. "Remember what Sunil said about those construction guys disappearing?"

Ravine nodded. He made a good point. Only, how would they figure that out when they could both see the house and see each other standing by the house? How would they know if no one could see them? And what if they really did disappear?

Between them, they had it all worked out by the time they got home.

They stopped in front of Derek's house. "Do you think you'll be able to go out tonight?" he asked.

Ravine smiled. Of course she could. Her parents were strict, but as long as she was home before dark and she was with Derek, it wouldn't be a problem.

"Good. I'll meet you in front of the Morgans' house at seven, and we'll go over there together," Derek said.

"Okay," Ravine replied. "But don't be late, Derek. I'm not standing in front of their place all night looking like a dork."

"I'll call you if plans change," he said, walking to his front door.

"You better!"

Ravine ran the rest of the way home with her backpack bumping up and down on her shoulders. Derek was her best friend, but he had a terrible habit of standing her up. She knew it was never on purpose. He'd get lost in a video game or something on the computer; then he'd spend the next day apologizing and explaining how he finally beat a level, or shot down a bad guy, or won a hockey game against the best team.

"I'm home," she yelled, as she opened the front door. She flung her stuff on the floor in the foyer and went into the kitchen. Her mother was watching the Cuisine Channel and trying to cook whatever it was they were making on television. Something smelled burnt, and Ravine guessed it wasn't burnt on the TV show.

"Hi, Ravine. Can you hand me the angel hair pasta, please? It's on the table behind you."

This was the first time in quite a while that her mother had turned on the television to watch the Cuisine Channel. That used to be normal for her, even though she usually ruined whatever recipe she was trying to follow. So Ravine was a little surprised to find her cooking away. But she was disappointed to find that it wasn't going so well, just like normal.

"What are you making?" she asked suspiciously, handing her mother the big plastic bag.

"A noodle pudding."

"Oh," said Ravine. That sounded disgusting.

Suddenly Ravine yelled at her mother. "Mom! The pot is on fire!"

Her mother whirled around, arms flying in every direction like a stressed-out octopus. She found the baking soda and poured it over the scorched noodles, smothering the flames. Finally, when the fire had been extinguished, her mother flopped into a chair and groaned.

"Well, I guess we'll have to order pizza tonight," she said sadly, looking at her soggy, burnt noodle pudding. She leaned her elbows on the table and turned toward Ravine with a weak smile.

"Who wants to eat noodle pudding anyway? It probably tastes horrible. Even without the baking soda," Ravine said. Her mother laughed. A laugh. That was something she hadn't heard from her mother in a long time.

They both looked at the burnt pot.

"What were you thinking?" Ravine asked, laughing. "Noodle pudding? That doesn't even sound like food."

Her mother shook her head, chuckling, and put her arm around Ravine. Ravine liked the sound of her mother laughing.

Ravine hugged her back and then started to clean up while her mother flipped through the phone book to order dinner.

Ravine could eat pizza three times a day, seven days a week, so she was glad supper was botched.

Ravine asked her mother to call her when dinner arrived, then grabbed her knapsack and headed up to her room, locking the door behind her. She walked to the window. Number 56 was still there, and she found herself staring at the mysterious house.

The old yellow bricks took on a kind of glow in the late afternoon sun, but the house still seemed to be brooding. The wooden shingles were cracked, and a few were missing. The paint on the shutters was blistered and peeled, and the rickety wrap-around verandah was falling away from the house in some places.

The windows were especially gloomy and seemed to be looking out on the world like angry, shrunken eyes. The old curtains blew in the wind that whooshed through the broken panes of glass. But the only time light seemed to enter or leave the house was when some invisible hand switched the lights on and off.

On and off. That wasn't happening right now, but as Ravine stood looking at the house, it seemed to lean closer, as if it were calling to her.

Just then, a chill ran down her spine, and she thought she could feel cold fingers touching her shoulder. She spun around, terrified. But no one was there; she was alone. She sat down on her bed, shivering.

Derek dropped his backpack on the floor in the kitchen and headed straight for the fridge. He stuck his head in the crisper and yelled, "What's there to eat?" He didn't hear his mother come quietly into the kitchen. She stood behind him with her arms crossed over her chest while he slammed the fridge door, disappointed that there was never anything good to eat in this house.

He jumped like a startled cat when he saw his mother.

"We have lots of good things to eat. They're called fruits and vegetables," his mother said.

Derek made a sour face. "What's for supper?" he asked, wondering if it was something he should save his appetite for.

"Spaghetti."

"I'll wait until supper," he said and walked out of the kitchen, still hungry.

He heard his older sister in the living room talking on the phone, and he thought about going in there and bugging her, just for the heck of it. But he decided against it; he couldn't do anything that might wreck his chances of going out after supper.

Derek headed to his room. He would have less chance of getting into trouble if he stayed out of everybody's way.

As he closed the door behind him, he went to the window and stared across the street. Even in the sunshine, the house looked dark and eerie.

Just as he was about to step away from the window, he felt a sharp, cold hand touch his shoulder, and he quickly jerked around. No one was there.

Chapter Four

Ravine stood on the sidewalk in front of the Morgan house waiting for Derek; he was already ten minutes late. Oh, she was going to strangle him when he got here.

She shifted her weight from foot to foot. "I'll give him five minutes more," she thought. Then she would go home, call him on the phone, and yell at him.

She looked at the invisible house. Well, invisible to everyone but her and Derek. It was almost the same time as it had been the previous night when she and Derek had first noticed the lights turning on and off. She was straining to see into the window with the torn curtain when, suddenly, the lights inside began to flicker again.

On. Off. On. Off.

The same as last night. When the flickering stopped, Ravine could hear her heart pounding inside her chest.

"What do you think that was?" Derek whispered, as he came up beside her. He had seen the lights and felt the same anxiety.

Not having heard him approach, Ravine jumped at the sound of his voice.

"I don't know," she said softly, forgetting that she was angry with him. They stood glued to the sidewalk, staring at the house for what seemed to be a long time, although it was really only a couple of minutes.

"Ready?" Derek asked.

"Yes."

Derek glanced at Ravine, but she was still staring at the house. The wind suddenly picked up and howled in their ears. The yellow brick house drew them in, urging them toward the old porch. There seemed to be the sound of crying in the wind that grew louder as the house beckoned them closer. As if unable to resist, Ravine and Derek headed up the long walk toward 56 Water Street.

Struck with a sudden urge to run home, Derek debated holding Ravine's hand. But he didn't want to look like a sissy, so he shoved his hands in his pockets, trying to look cool and confident. He couldn't let Ravine know he was scared out of his wits. He would never have admitted it out loud, but he knew he wasn't as brave as her.

He stole another glance at Ravine, who appeared to be a lot more confident than he felt. If he had looked more carefully, he might have noticed she was unsteady on her feet and was biting her lip. But not much seemed to scare Ravine, Derek thought.

They walked slowly, and when their feet finally stepped onto the scruffy lawn, they vanished.

Carefully, they walked up the cracked stairs of the rotting porch. As they neared the front door, the wooden boards beneath their feet screeched as if in pain. They looked at each other, both wondering if this was a warning.

The paint on the front door had peeled, and what remained was so badly faded that Derek and Ravine could only guess what colour it had been. The bricks at the front of the house were crumbling, allowing the wind to whistle through the cracks. If they had looked closely, which neither of them did, they would have seen tiny black spiders spinning webs between the bricks, collecting caches of suffocated insects. Many of the floor boards were missing; most that remained were beginning to rot. Derek and Ravine moved slowly, being careful to avoid the weakest-looking boards.

The wind picked up again, blowing Ravine's hair around her face, and the air turned chilly as it whistled in her ears and around her head. The old weeping willow waved furiously, stretching its long branches toward them as though it wanted to engulf them. The shadows on the weathered trunk were shaped like drooping eyes and a twisted mouth that seemed to be crying out, warning them to stay away.

Ravine and Derek took deep breaths.

As suddenly as it had started, the wind stopped, and the cold air disappeared. Derek and Ravine looked at each other, waiting for their heartbeats to return to normal. As their intense panic eased, a healthy fear of the unknown and a curiosity about what they would encounter behind the door remained.

Derek turned to look at the activity on the street. It was pretty much the same as last night. But as he watched friends and neighbours enjoying the final hours before bed, he realized that no one was paying attention to them. Sunil and Joannie were looking straight at them, but there was no response when he waved.

"They can't see us," said Ravine.

Derek called to Joannie and Sunil in his loudest voice, but they didn't notice. No one else responded to him, either. The residents of Water Street continued on with their own business, not even seeing Ravine and Derek.

The two stood facing each other, realizing what their friends had said was true. People who came to this place disappeared. There was no house, and there was no Derek and Ravine. At least not to anyone else.

"I guess that answers our question," Derek choked out, shaken. Until tonight, a small part of him thought their friends were playing a joke on them, getting caught up in the excitement of the supernatural. Now he realized why both their parents had been so worried. A sick feeling settled in his stomach, and for a brief moment he thought he might throw up.

"Yes, I guess it does," she said.

Feeling the bile rise from his stomach into his throat, Derek swallowed hard to keep himself from barfing. He wished he was back at home, sitting in front of his computer, far away from this house. But he was not going to be the first to chicken out.

Slowly reaching for the door knob and gripping firmly, Derek turned it and pushed the door with all his body weight. To his surprise, it opened easily, and he went flying through the door, stumbling over his feet and landing flat on his stomach.

"Are you okay?" Ravine asked, rushing to kneel beside him. She helped him up as he brushed himself off. His face and pants were covered in a film of light, silky dust. He coughed a couple of times and wiped his cheek with the back of his hand.

"Well, whoever lives here should definitely clean more often," he said.

Ravine smiled at his joke and would have laughed but her vocal chords seemed to be temporarily disabled.

The house was dark.

It was darker than dark.

Though the curtains were torn and ragged, no light seemed to come through the windows. Even the light from the open door seemed to stop at the threshold. If they looked away from the door into the room, they could not see their hands in front of their faces.

They both shivered.

The house was cold.

It was colder than cold.

It felt as though they had just walked into a huge freezer.

The house was quiet.

It was quieter than quiet.

The only sound they could hear was the beating of their own hearts. Nothing else in the house made any noise.

Until all the dust he had kicked up when he stumbled caused Derek to explode in a huge sneeze that sent echoes running through the quiet. It seemed to be unnaturally loud, and he hoped he hadn't woken anything that would be better left sleeping.

They reached for each other at the same time and, holding hands, took a couple of steps into the blackness of the invisible house.

"I guess we should have brought a flashlight," Derek said, sniffing. He was afraid to sneeze and disturb the silence again.

"And jackets," Ravine whispered, shivering in the chilly air.

They walked further into the house with their hands in front of them to lead the way. Suddenly, a whistling sound went flying by their heads, and they froze. The sound intensified, getting louder and closer, until cold, boney hands touched their shoulders.

Derek and Ravine stumbled backward and, without hesitation, they went tearing out of the house. The door was still open, and they flew down the steps, running as fast as their legs could carry them toward the Morgan house. To safer ground.

Still panting, partly because of fright and partly because of the run, Derek bent down, trying to catch his breath. The warm summer air soon revived him.

Ravine sat on the grass, breathing heavily and trying to clear the mist from her glasses. It had been so cold inside the house that the warm summer air had fogged them.

Derek looked up and saw Sunil and Joannie waving to them. He waved back faintly, but his arms felt heavy. As he watched Ravine's breathing slowly return to normal, he realized how very tired he was. His legs felt cumbersome and his feet felt sluggish. He could see beads of sweat dampening Ravine's forehead, and her cheeks were red and heated.

"What time is it?" she asked, wiping her brow.

Derek sat down beside her. He checked his watch, then shook his head and put his wrist up to his ear.

"What's wrong?" Ravine asked.

"Don't know. My watch still says the same time it did when we went into the house. It's like we never went in. Or time stood still. Or it never even happened, or something."

He looked at Ravine as he realized the significance of his words.

"Not possible. Let me see that," Ravine said, yanking Derek's arm toward her. Sure enough, he was right. It was exactly twenty past seven.

"Maybe there's something wrong with your watch?" she said doubtfully, lifting Derek's arm to her ear.

"Maybe," Derek said, "but I don't think so."

"It's still ticking," she said, pushing the watch close to his ear.

They sat on the lawn for a few minutes watching their friends play across the street. The longer they sat, the less real the experience inside the house seemed. After a while, they had to ask each other if they had really gone inside. The memory was fading quickly, but Derek's pants were still covered in a thick layer of dust and ground-in dirt, so they knew it had been real.

Sunil and Joannie crossed the street to where Derek and Ravine were sitting.

"What are you guys doing?" Joannie asked. "Didn't you hear us calling?" Without waiting for an answer, she added: "Sunil and me are going to the park. Do you wanna come?"

Ravine was tired, as if she had just run a marathon. Her legs and chest ached. All she wanted was to go home and slip into her soft bed. If she could make it that far.

"I can't. I promised my mom I would clean my room tonight, and she said if I didn't, I would be grounded the first week of summer vacation," Ravine lied.

"What about you, dude?" Sunil asked Derek.

Derek wanted someone to carry him home. He was too tired to walk and most certainly too tired to explain his filthy pants to his mother. He sighed. Brand new, cream-coloured summer pants. "Mom is going to be furious," he thought.

"I think I'm going home, too," Derek said, and he stood up.

"Dude! What's up with your pants? They look new," Sunil said, "except for the dirt."

Derek looked down at his pants. "I fell in a mud puddle," he said.

"Mud?" Joannie asked. "Where would you find mud? It hasn't rained for weeks."

Ravine and Derek looked at each other, but all Derek could come up with was, "Just a mud puddle over there." He pointed off vaguely over his shoulder.

Joannie and Sunil shrugged.

"Okay. Catch ya later," Sunil said.

Ravine and Derek watched their friends head to the park. Joannie looked back at them and, as she and Sunil passed 56 Water Street, she playfully pushed Sunil toward the lawn saying, "Oooh, be careful. You don't want to disappear forever!"

Sunil pushed her back and chased her the rest of the way down the street.

"If they only knew," Ravine muttered.

"They have no idea."

They crossed the street and walked home in silence.

Ravine opened her front door and mouthed a silent hello as she passed her parents. It took all her energy to crawl up the stairs to her room.

She flopped onto her bed without changing into her pajamas. She tried to stare out the window, but her eyes slowly closed. Just as she drifted into sleep, she heard a quiet whisper.

"Come back, Ravine. Do not leave me. Come back …"

Derek opened the front door and poked his head around the corner. The coast was clear; his mother must be in the kitchen. He began to climb the stairs, yelling, "I'm home. I'm going to bed."

He slipped into his room and got into his pajamas, hiding his dirty pants at the back of his closet, underneath a Monopoly game. That would at least buy him some time. Maybe she would never find them, he thought, as he climbed into bed.

"You're in bed early," his mom said, opening his bedroom door.

"Yeah, I'm tired." he said, closing his eyes.

Derek felt her hand on his forehead. "You don't feel warm," she said. "Maybe you are just tired from the heat." She gave him a kiss and then went to open his window.

"There should be a nice, cooling breeze tonight," she said and left the room, closing the door behind her.

Once again, the wind picked up, and Derek could feel it circling his head. Then, just as he fell asleep, he was sure he heard somebody whispering.

"Come back, Derek. Do not leave me. Come back …"

Chapter Five

The next two days went by quickly. Ravine and Derek spent more time organizing the carnival than doing school work. No one studied much during the last week of school anyway. Everyone's focus was on the carnival and on making it the biggest year-end fundraiser ever.

Even though the days passed quickly, Derek and Ravine had restless nights. Their sleep was disturbed by strange dreams filled with eerie cries and whispers. They managed to talk a little on their way to and from school, but they were exhausted, so mostly they just complained about their lack of sleep and their dreams.

There was no time for Derek and Ravine to make any plans to go back to the invisible house. They were too involved with the carnival, deciding where to set up the tent for Madame Jewels, making posters, organizing ticket sales, and making a fortune-telling schedule for Madame. It was a lot of work, but the distraction was exactly what they needed.

Everybody was preoccupied with the carnival. Sunil and Joannie were in charge of the candy floss machine, and Lisa and Deborah were arranging the water balloon toss. A couple of kids in another class had convinced the music teacher and the gym teacher to be on the receiving end of a whipped cream pie toss. A lot of kids were looking forward to that opportunity!

All the activity was getting lots of attention, but it was Ravine and Derek's mysterious lady who had everybody excited. Students from all grades inquired about the cost to have their fortunes read. Madame Jewels was going to be a big success.

Ravine hung time schedules outside the washrooms, and the fortune teller's time was almost booked within just a few hours. Madame Jewels said each reading would be ten minutes long, and she wanted a break halfway through the afternoon.

She promised Ravine and Derek that she would save enough time to read their fortunes, too.

Today was Thursday, and tomorrow was the big day. One more day, the carnival, and then they would be on summer vacation.

Derek and Ravine had agreed to stay away from Number 56 until school was over. Derek planned to spend some time with his computer researching the Ruperts or Roberts. Although he and Ravine had no ideas about why they could see this house when no one else could, finding some information about the people who used to live there seemed like it might provide some clues.

Ravine sat in class and turned her attention to the open window. A butterfly was hovering just outside, almost close enough to touch.

Mrs. Tackle was chattering about the carnival, repeating herself like a broken record. But at this point in the school year, she was only putting in time until vacation, just like her students. Nattering endlessly about the carnival was better than trying to teach a group of kids whose minds were somewhere else.

Ravine knew that no one was really listening, except probably Derek; he usually paid close attention to Mrs. Tackle. She wished the teacher would just dismiss everyone for the rest of the day. Thankfully, tomorrow was the carnival.

While Ravine idly watched the butterfly, she thought about Madame Jewels. The woman seemed so nice on the phone, and Ravine wondered if she might be able to tell them anything about 56 Water Street. After all, a fortune teller is supposed to know lots of mysterious stuff.

Ravine forced herself to stop thinking about the house.

Tomorrow was also report card day, and she smiled at that thought. She was one of the smartest kids in her class, and she actually liked report card day.

She continued to watch the butterfly and let her mind drift to thoughts of summer vacation. She was going to sleep late every day.

Derek sat at his desk, resting his head on his hand and trying to listen to Mrs. Tackle. He always tried to pay attention to her. But she looked as bored as he felt.

His mind drifted, and he began thinking about the carnival. "Was Madame Jewels a real fortune teller or just a hoax?" he wondered. He wasn't sure if he really believed in spooky stuff. But if there was anything to it, he hoped she might actually know about the supernatural. In fact, maybe she would be able to see the house, too.

As his mind wandered, his doodling started to take shape. At first, he wasn't too sure what he was drawing, but the farther his thoughts ranged, the more the pencil took on a mind of its own, and the faster he sketched. He was creating a gloomy picture that was obviously the house at 56 Water Street. He quickly filled the page.

It was a large two-and-a-half storey faced with yellow bricks. Turrets on either side seemed to reach to the sky. Long, vertical windows lined the front of the house, and a porch wrapped all the way around. The windows at the front were broken, but it was clear from the few remaining shards that some of the glass had originally been stained. The porch was ramshackle and leaned precariously away from the foundation.

The old house showed its age, but it was easy to see that it had once been grand and stately. In fact, Derek realized that some of what he had drawn was not what he and Ravine had seen; he had obviously reproduced some parts of it as they must have looked years ago.

Derek had masterfully captured the house on paper. He had included the old willow and, even in his sketch, the branches seemed to be reaching out toward him.

Staring at the picture, he felt as if he could climb inside the drawing and disappear forever. The thought terrified him. He had drawn the image much faster than he usually sketched, but he had still captured all the details so clearly; the house seemed so real. He ran his hand slowly across the sketch, as though he could touch the house. But nothing happened.

He continued adding little touches and was lost in the world of his sketch. So he didn't hear Mrs. Tackle call his name. And he didn't see her coming until her hand slid across his picture and took it away from him.

"What's this, Derek?" Mrs. Tackle asked.

"Just a picture," he muttered, embarrassed at being caught. He always doodled or sketched in class, but he was usually able to cover it up in time if the teacher came by.

She walked back to the front of the class and put the notebook on her desk. "You can have this back after class," she said and then continued talking to the class about the carnival like there had not been any distraction.

Derek looked up at the clock. Only fifteen minutes until home time. Only fifteen minutes more of this day, he thought. And he would get his notebook back.

He turned his attention to the open window. A butterfly was floating nearby, almost close enough to touch. He picked up his pencil to sketch the butterfly but then remembered Mrs. Tackle had taken away his notebook, and he put the pencil down.

The bell rang, and everyone jumped from their seats like a bunch of frogs with their butts on fire. As they rushed out the door, Mrs. Tackle called after them to remember everything they needed for tomorrow's carnival.

Derek walked up to her desk, and she handed the closed notebook back to him.

"Excellent picture, Derek, but you do need to pay attention in class, even when no one else does," she added, glancing at Ravine. Then she reached into her desk and handed something to him. "You might want to consider this. It's a drawing contest, and the winner gets to spend a week with Mike Markle, the man who illustrates the Bobby Bunches books."

Derek took the pamphlet, opened it, and read the contest rules. He was instantly excited, and his mind started racing about what he should draw. He couldn't believe it. Mike Markle! What a great opportunity. The Bobby Bunches detective mysteries were very popular with kids these days. They were especially famous for their illustrations.

"Thanks, Mrs. Tackle," Derek said. "You're the best!"

Mrs. Tackle smiled. She liked all her students, but she really liked Derek, and she knew he had a gift that was worth encouraging. She walked to the door. "I'll see you two tomorrow," she said as she left.

Ravine stood beside Derek, looking at the pamphlet. "You're going to win," she said, "I just know it!"

Maybe he'd enter the picture of the house he just drew. He thought it was probably one of his best drawings. He opened his notebook and flipped through the pages to find it.

He flipped slowly. Then he flipped fast. Then slowly again. He set the notebook on Mrs. Tackle's desk, flipping through the pages one by one.

"What's wrong, Derek?" Ravine asked, following him back to the teacher's desk.

"It's not here," Derek said, shaking his head.

"What's not?"

"The picture I just drew of the house. It's not here."

"Maybe Mrs. Tackle threw it in the garbage," Ravine said, bending over and going through the crumpled papers in the wastebasket.

Derek shook his head. "Nah, Mrs. Tackle would never do that. She doesn't even throw out the notes that get passed around. She always gives them back. Besides, there is no place where she tore out a piece of paper."

Derek and Ravine stared at each other.

As they walked home, they were quiet. Finally Ravine said, "You think she's pretty, don't you?"

"Huh? Who?" Derek asked.

"Mrs. Tackle. You think she's pretty. It's a good thing she didn't notice the sketches of her in your book."

Derek blushed. Then he laughed out loud, a little too loud, and muttered something about what a load of nonsense that was.

They continued on in silence for a while until Derek finally said, "Well, she is pretty."

That evening, Ravine went to Derek's house to work on a sign for the fortune teller's exhibit. She knocked on his bedroom door, and he yelled to her to come in.

"I brought the markers, glitter glue, and Bristol board." She held up a large piece of fluorescent pink Bristol board, but Derek wasn't paying attention.

"Come here," he said. "Take a look at this."

Ravine moved closer to his chair and stood behind him, looking over his shoulder. She watched as he drew a picture of the house across the road so fast that the pencil seemed to move on its own. When he was done, he put the charcoal down and closed the notebook, keeping his finger in the page with the drawing. He waited a couple of seconds and then opened the notebook.

The picture was gone.

He picked up the pencil again and drew the house with the same speed as before, repeating the process.

The picture was gone again.

He tried it again, and then again. But each time, the picture disappeared.

"Whoa!" Ravine said, her eyes bugging out of her head. "Whoa!"

"Now watch this," he said.

He drew the picture once more, and put the pencil down. They both looked at the sketch, but nothing happened.

"See how it doesn't disappear?" Derek asked.

Ravine nodded.

"Now watch this," he said. Without closing the notebook, he turned himself and Ravine so their backs were to the picture. When they turned around again, it was gone.

They looked at each other, mystified.

Derek leaned over his desk and pulled the curtain back from the window and looked at the house that loomed over the street. The air was warm and still, but a cold chill came through the open window, and the weeping willow seemed to sway wildly and gesture to them with its branches.

Suddenly cold, Derek closed the window.

Ravine shivered.

Chapter Six

Ravine awoke early on Friday morning. She knew she had dreamt about the house, but she couldn't remember anything about it. The memory hovered just beyond her reach, but she couldn't grasp the details. She had a strong sense that it hadn't felt like a dream while it was happening. It felt more like someone had pulled her into a world far away from the one she lived in, a world that was not hers.

She was tired and dressed absentmindedly before heading downstairs.

The last day of school was always the best day of the year. She liked it even better than Christmas, and she was looking forward to the carnival. She knew that would wake her up.

"Hi, sweetheart. Is that you?" Ravine heard her mother call to her from the kitchen. Ravine shook her head; a dumb question deserved a dumb answer.

"No, Mom, it's Albert Einstein," she said, sitting down at the table.

Her mother bent over and gave her a kiss on the cheek. "Very funny. What would Albert Einstein like for breakfast? And why does he have his shirt on inside out?"

"Just toast. I don't have much time. Derek and I need to be at school a bit early today to get the tent ready for Madame Jewels."

Her mother nodded as Ravine put her shirt on the right way. Summer vacation had finally arrived, and Ravine's mother sat down to remind her daughter about the summer vacation rules.

"I'll get your toast ready in a minute, sweetheart. I need you to listen to me carefully, okay? Now, when your father and I are working, I want you to remember some important rules. It's a big responsibility being here by yourself. When you wake up, you call Derek's mom to let her know you are okay. Mrs. Radley said that you are welcome to have lunch over there on days that you are here alone—"

"Awww, Mom, I know how to get my own lunch."

"Those are the rules, Ravine. You also need to be home by five o'clock. And you must let Derek's mom know where you are at all times. Understand?"

Ravine nodded. She understood. She understood that her mother was afraid to let her go and do things, kid things. She also understood why. Ravine knew that her mother would eventually relax a bit, and she was willing to wait for that without complaining too much about rules and curfews. Ravine missed her sister, too.

"Also, don't forget your key. But if you do, Mrs. Radley has a spare. And remember to lock the doors all the time. Especially when you're home. Okay?"

Ravine nodded again, and her mother smiled, relieved.

"You are very responsible, Ravine. I know I can trust you. It's just everyone else I worry about."

Her mother got up, straightened out her dress, and started to make the toast. She worked today, so that meant Ravine had to come directly home from school.

Ravine ate her toast quickly, then gave her mom a little hug and left to enjoy the last day of school.

Derek tumbled out of bed and got dressed, still tired. He had spent a lot of time after Ravine went home the previous night drawing pictures of the house and watching them disappear. He got little sleep. Thank goodness he could sleep in tomorrow, he thought.

He knew Ravine's mom worked today, so they wouldn't be able to go to the house after school. He was reluctant to go back there at night anyway; it could wait until tomorrow.

Heading downstairs, he could hear his mother and sister arguing in the kitchen. He sat down at the table, and his mom greeted him with a bowl of cereal. He turned his nose up. Boring old Rice Krispies again. He thought about complaining but changed his mind.

His mother and sister had stopped arguing when he walked into the kitchen, and his sister was at the table, looking sullen and miserable. Whatever Danielle had done last night had really ticked his mother off, so he thought it would be better to keep his mouth shut.

Derek finished his breakfast and left the house just as his mother and Danielle started arguing again. He didn't wait to find out what the fight was about.

As he opened the front door, he saw Ravine standing at the end of the drive-way waiting for him. He ran down the steps and quickly noticed that she looked as tired as he felt. They headed off to school, barely talking and only half-awake.

"Your socks don't match," he said.

The school yard was buzzing. Teachers and students were setting up displays, games, activities, and food stands for the carnival. For the first time all week, Derek forgot about the invisible house.

Students and teachers spent the early morning hanging up signs and decorating the playground. The carnival started at ten o'clock, and everyone was ready for it to begin and eager for summer vacation to start. It was hard to tell which excited them more.

The day was warm and sunny, perfect for a carnival. Not too hot, not a cloud in the sky, with a nice light breeze to keep everything fresh.

Derek and Ravine walked around the playground. They had already spent a couple of hours sitting in front of their fortune teller's tent, selling and collecting tickets.

The line for Madame Jewels was the longest in the schoolyard. The schedules that Derek and Ravine posted had been filled for a couple of days, but even some kids who had not signed up were there, hoping they might get a chance if someone else didn't show up. Everybody wanted their fortune read. Madame Jewels was a big hit.

When she had arrived in the morning with her own tent and all her own equipment, Ravine and Derek had helped her set it up. It looked like a regular tent, the kind you would take to go camping. But it was made out of a light material that felt silky and reminded Ravine of satin bed sheets, and the tent was definitely not the colour of a camping tent. It was navy blue, with glittery gold stars; it had a door made of long strings of blue and gold beads.

In front of the tent, Madame Jewels had put up a blue standing board with her name printed in large, bold, glittery letters. For the past couple of hours, there had been a steady stream of kids coming and going to get their fortunes read. Even a few teachers entered the tent.

Madame finally came out, smiling but looking tired. It was time for her break, and she strolled over to buy a hot dog. Her deep blue skirt rustled and flirted around her ankles so that she looked as if she was gliding, not walking. Derek and Ravine watched her with great interest. Madame's jewelry kept up a clanging rhythm as she crossed the schoolyard, and the sun reflected off her large hoop earrings. When she turned her head the right way, it looked as if she was walking in her own halo of light. Everyone stopped to stare. Even the teachers seemed fascinated with this mysterious lady.

Derek wished the carnival would be over soon so they could get their turn to have their fortunes read. But with Madame on break, they decided to check out the activities.

"Let's go see the balloon toss," Ravine said.

At the balloon toss, two lines were drawn on the pavement five feet apart. Derek and Ravine stood on the lines, each holding a balloon full of water. The idea of the game was to see who could get their opponent wetter than they got themselves. And contestants had to stand with their toes on those lines, not moving their feet.

Lisa was in charge of the balloons; she raised her flag and blew a horn to start the game. Contestants had thirty balloons each and sixty seconds to throw as many of them as they could.

Ravine got hit a few times even though she swerved from side to side trying to avoid Derek's balloons. All that motion made it pretty hard to throw her own balloons, but she did hit Derek a few times. Derek leaned backward to avoid one throw and fell onto a balloon that had missed him earlier. By this time, they were laughing so hard they didn't hear Lisa yelling that time was up.

"That was fun," Derek said, shaking his hair like a wet dog.

Ravine wiped her wet face with her wet sleeve, but it didn't help much. They were both soaked.

After that, they wandered to some of the other activities, hoping the warm sun would dry them. At the pie toss, they watched as kids consistently failed to hit the teachers.

Ravine rolled her eyes at an older boy who hadn't come within five feet of either teacher. "That is so pathetic," she told him. "You're curving your arm; that's why you keep missing."

Ravine shook her head when he missed again. "Oh, here, let me show you."

She gave Annie two bucks for a pie and then nailed Mr. Platt right in the face with a perfect throw.

"That's how you do it," she said.

The music teacher licked the cream off his face with his tongue.

"Good pie, Mr. Platt?" asked the gym teacher, trying to turn his head to see.

"Yes, Mr. Scott. Good pie. You'll enjoy being hit yourself. Going to make quite mess of your beard, though."

Derek and Ravine then went to the three-legged-race area. Joannie and Sunil were at the starting line with their legs already tied.

"Hurry up, you guys," Sunil yelled to them. "They're starting in two minutes."

Ravine and Derek ran to the starting line and tied a bandana around their legs.

"Dude, we are going to kick your butts," Sunil said, laughing.

"In your dreams," said Ravine.

Halfway through the race, Derek tripped over his untied shoe lace. He fell to the ground, dragging Ravine with him. They struggled to get back up and still managed to finish in third place, despite being unable to catch their breath through their laughter.

"Good race, man!" Sunil showed off the first place ribbon around his neck.

Derek and Ravine went to the food booth and bought hot dogs and candy floss. Then they sat by the school fence with their snacks, watching the activity.

They watched as Sunil's pie went far wide of either teacher.

"See the way Sunil throws?" asked Derek, with a laugh. "He throws like a girl."

Ravine gave him a dirty look. "What do you mean, he throws like a girl? I didn't see you nail the teacher. But I did."

"Yeah, but you don't throw like a girl. You throw better than anybody I know," Derek explained.

"Oh. Okay, then." She watched Sunil again and laughed when the pie slipped out of his hand and landed by his feet.

They sat by the fence a bit longer, enjoying the afternoon. Then, through all the commotion, they saw Madame Jewels glide back toward the tent. Ravine was about to jump up when she noticed Derek was staring at Mrs. Tackle, who was by the hot dog stand. In her pretty summer dress, she looked even better than usual. Ravine poked Derek to signal it was time to go back to work.

Chapter Seven

After the last scheduled fortune was read, Derek and Ravine slipped into the tent. It was their turn now, and they sat at the round wooden table that was just big enough for three small chairs.

Madame Jewels smiled at them. She took the crystal ball off the table and placed it in a black velvet box by her feet. Then she took off her colourful head-band with its attached long, black wig and removed her flashy costume jewelry. She placed them neatly in a small navy trunk with gold stars. She unsnapped her long, sparkly blue skirt and put that in the trunk, too. Slipping the blouse over her head and shaking her hair, Madame neatly folded the garment and placed it in the trunk on top of her skirt.

Derek and Ravine found themselves looking at an ordinary woman in an ordinary white T-shirt and ordinary blue shorts. Her hair was blond and hung past her shoulders in tight curls. Her blue eyes, pencil-thin lips, straight nose, and fair complexion added to her ordinariness. She didn't seem mysterious anymore.

Madame Jewels looked like she could be somebody's big sister or mother. Even worse, she looked like she could work at the corner grocery store. Ravine looked at Derek and could see he was disappointed.

Madame was no longer the exotic, mystifying vision she had been when she first walked onto the school grounds.

"What are you doing?" Derek asked. "Why are you putting all your stuff away? Aren't you going to read our fortunes?"

Madame Jewels sat across from Derek and Ravine.

"You can call me Madeline. That's my first name. Jewels is my real last name. And, yes, I'm going to give you two a reading."

"Then why did you put all your stuff away?" Derek asked.

"Because this stuff isn't real. It's hokey. Kids your age like all the glitter and stuff, especially the crystal ball. But that's all for show, and something tells me you two don't need all that."

She looked at the disappointed expression on the boy sitting across from her. It wasn't an unexpected reaction, but she was a little surprised that the girl seemed to be taking this all in stride. Madeline needed to talk to these two children about their special gifts without the distraction of her stage costume. She had some important information to share with them.

"So you're really not a fortune teller?" Derek asked.

Madeline shook her head. "No, I'm not a fortune teller; I'm not even sure there really are authentic fortune tellers. But I am a psychic. And a medium."

"I was really looking forward to getting my fortune read," said Derek. He sounded so disappointed.

"What are psychics and mediums?" Ravine asked.

"A psychic is a person who can read people's feelings and know things other people can't possibly know," Madeline said. "A medium is a person who can communicate with spirits and ghosts."

Derek looked at Ravine. She didn't seem to be disappointed like him. But he thought this psychic and medium stuff sounded a lot hokier than the crystal ball and glittery costume. Those things seemed far more interesting.

Madame Jewels was prepared for this. She knew it didn't sound interesting. Not yet, anyway.

"Has anyone ever told either of you that you have wonderful imaginations?" Madeline asked.

Both kids nodded.

"I believe what both of you have is a special gift that has allowed you to see things that others can't see. Or won't see. Or are just too scared to see."

Derek and Ravine sat very still.

Ravine knew she saw things that other people did not see, but she had been keeping these things to herself for a long time. She and Derek shared the mystery house across the street, but she hadn't even told him about the other things she had seen. Not yet.

Ravine squirmed in her chair. This was getting a little uncomfortable. If Madeline was talking to both of them, maybe she knew something about them and Number 56. But how could this woman know they had been seeing things that no one else saw?

"You see spirits and ghosts," Madeline said. "You see images that most people don't see, and you hear things most people don't hear. You can unveil the spirit world and bring it closer to our own world."

Derek and Ravine stared at her.

Madeline sat and quietly observed the kids. "Does this make sense to either of you?" she asked.

Ravine nodded. Derek shook his head.

"I know this house …" she said. "A big house … a special house …"

Derek and Ravine sat taller in their chairs.

"I see 56 Water Street, too," she said, waiting to take her next cue from the kids.

"You see it, too?" they said together.

"We thought we were the only ones who could see it," Ravine said.

"It's really creepy and scary inside," Derek blurted out.

"I was walking around the neighbourhood one night," Madeline said, "and saw the two of you climbing the stairs to the porch. I saw you open the front door and, a few minutes later, you ran back out with looks of fear on your faces."

Madeline took each of their hands. "And I guessed what you must have encountered. You have nothing to be scared of. Isabel Roberts can't hurt you."

"Isabel Roberts?" they said together.

"I know you have heard her; or maybe you've even seen her. I have gone into the house so many times to try and find her, but she will not show herself to me. I know she's there; I can feel her energy. Maybe she doesn't trust me. I don't know. She is the first one I have not been able to help. To send back to the light."

Ravine and Derek stared at Madeline, open mouthed. This was a lot stranger than any crystal ball. There was nothing ordinary about the woman sitting across from them in the ordinary clothes.

"I moved here six months ago," Madeline continued, "and when I was looking for a place to live, I came across 56 Water Street. It attracted my interest, although I didn't know why at the time. When I looked into it, the real estate lady got mad at me and accused me of wasting her time. It took me a little while to catch on that she didn't think there was a house there at all. So I did some digging around and couldn't find anyone else who believed it was there either. That's when I realized the truth."

She paused to look at Derek and Ravine. "So I bought a house two blocks away and kept an eye on it. I have been inside fifty-six many times, but I have never been able to help Isabel. She trusts you two, and you need to help her go home. That's why you hear her calling to you and why you can see her. I know you can, or you wouldn't have run out of the house in fright."

Madeline stopped and placed one hand over Ravine's hands and another over Derek's. "Isabel wants your help, and she is confused. She might not even remember she is dead. I'm not sure why she's here, but that's where you two come in; that's why she seems willing to reveal herself to you."

Ravine and Derek's eyes were as big and round as pancakes.

"What do you mean, she doesn't remember she's dead? How can you not remember you're dead?" Derek finally asked. This was all getting to be too much for him to absorb.

"She's been in a ghostly state for over a hundred years. I'm not sure what she remembers. But something is wrong in her world that prevents her from crossing over into the light. She's missing something or has lost something or is holding on to something. I don't know what, but that is the reason she hasn't crossed over."

"What does 'crossing over' mean?" Ravine asked. She was fascinated with Madeline and felt a connection with her. Finally, an adult who might understand all the strange things she saw and heard. This wasn't an ordinary woman at all. This was the most captivating and bewitching person Ravine had ever met.

"Crossing over means you travel into your true state of existence. We are spiritual beings, and we are only in these solid bodies for a short time. Our true identities lie on the other side. I guess there is no easy way to explain this, but if you think of it as crossing over to the afterlife, you'll have the idea."

Ravine nodded.

"Isabel wants you two to help her find whatever it is she's looking for. Every time I go into the house, she yells at me to go away. But because she lets you see her, I think she trusts you. Maybe it's because you're kids; she is only a child herself, maybe fifteen or sixteen. That might be why she thinks she can put her faith in you. But she doesn't have much time. If you want to help her, you need to get her to move to the light soon. Once she crosses over to the light, the house will disappear. Isabel has created the vision of the house, and it will fade away forever once she goes home. But she only has the strength to maintain the illusion for a short time."

"What do you mean by 'go home'?" Derek asked, confused and bewildered. His mind was racing, and he was only half listening to Madeline. It was the only way he could cope with this.

"She means heaven, you dummy," Ravine said, giving him a light punch in the arm.

Madeline nodded; that was exactly what she meant. "People call it different things, but heaven will do."

Derek told her about the disappearing picture he kept drawing.

Madeline nodded again. That was Isabel making it disappear. She wanted no one to see the house except the people she chose. Madeline was interested to learn that Mrs. Tackle had been able to see Derek's sketch.

"This is what she's trying to tell you. She wants you to understand that she is choosing to show you this house but can choose not to show it. Unless you have the special gift to communicate with the spiritual world, you can't see the image she has created. That's why no one else sees the house. When you sketched it, Derek, you brought it into the physical world where everyone else could see it; she doesn't want that for anyone except those she chooses."

Madeline paused.

"Do you understand what I just said?" she asked. "This is important, and not just because of Isabel. I told you a medium is someone who can communicate with ghosts or spirits. Like you. You two are mediums."

Derek and Ravine looked at each other. Derek gulped.

"Do you think it was a coincidence that of all the things you two could have done for your school carnival, you chose a fortune teller? And you chose me, someone who already knew two kids had recently been inside 56 Water Street."

They were all silent for a few minutes. Then Ravine asked Madeline where they could find information on Isabel Roberts. Madeline suggested they start in the archives of the *Eastern Times-News*. The only problem was Madeline didn't know the exact date of Isabel's death. She only knew it was sometime in the early 1900s.

"If you can connect with Isabel and get her home, you'll know because the house will disappear," Madeline said.

Ravine wanted to ask about her sister. Was Rachel hanging around? Had she crossed over? Was she okay? But the words just wouldn't come.

Derek and Ravine walked home in silence. Derek was still rattled by what Madeline had told them. But Madeline said they were on their own now; she couldn't help them anymore. It was up to them, and only they had the power to put Isabel at rest.

They agreed they would go back to the house Saturday morning, when it was light. Maybe the house would seem less frightening in the daytime.

In the meantime, Derek planned to search whatever news reports and city records about the property he could find online. Perhaps something interesting would turn up about Isabel.

When they got to Derek's house, neither of them bothered to say good-bye. They were too wrapped up in their own thoughts and fears about what lay ahead.

Chapter Eight

Ravine stood back watching and feeling as if she was standing at the narrow end of a long funnel. As the funnel gradually expanded, the secret world of the girl with the black hair and catlike eyes was opened to her.

The girl wore an old-fashioned, long, grey dress, and her hair was tied back with a ribbon. At least, Ravine *thought* the dress was grey. It was hard to be sure since everything seemed to be in shades of grey and white. Except for the girl's eyes. They were bright green, like a cat's eyes.

Ravine looked around her, and the images she saw were hazy and bleak. The girl did not walk; she floated. Her feet didn't move like she was taking real steps; she sort of hovered slightly above the ground and drifted gracefully.

Ravine felt as if she was being pulled through the funnel until she was in the same room as the girl. Ravine watched her drift by, calling out for someone named Sarah. It was obvious the girl was looking for Sarah, and Ravine wondered who that was.

As the girl floated up the stairs, Ravine followed just in time to see her disappear through a closed door. She seemed to have simply passed through the solid door, as if it wasn't there. Ravine walked toward the door and turned the handle slowly, gently pushing against it with her shoulder. It seemed solid enough to her, although it didn't strike her as strange that the girl had simply gone through it as if it weren't there. The door was either locked or stuck, and Ravine pushed it again, harder this time. It wouldn't open. She put her ear up to the door, but she could hear nothing.

She tried to speak, to call out to the girl, but when she opened her mouth, nothing came out.

Then, as Ravine was debating what to do next, the girl floated back through the closed door and moved down the stairway. As Ravine followed, she realized the girl had something in her hand, and Ravine hurried down the stairs, trying to catch up.

The figure floated around the living room, softly calling out to someone. Ravine couldn't quite hear, but she guessed it might still be Sarah. There was a look on the girl's face that could have been pain, or worry.

Abruptly, the girl disappeared through a wall, and Ravine opened the front door to find her standing beneath the willow tree.

Ravine watched and wondered if this was Isabel. She assumed it must be. The girl couldn't have been more than sixteen years old.

Ravine walked toward her slowly, trying to see what she was holding tight against her chest. But the girl paid no attention, floating past her and back into the house.

Ravine hurried back inside and found her sitting on the floor, still clutching something against her chest. Ravine stepped closer and reached out, but when she was almost close enough to touch her, the girl vanished.

Ravine stood in the middle of the room by herself. She looked down, and something on the floor caught her attention. She bent to pick it up. It was a stuffed bear, and Ravine grabbed it, holding it close to her own chest. It was soft and grey, like everything seemed to be.

Suddenly, she had the feeling she was falling.

As she rolled over and opened her eyes, Ravine realized she was in bed. She looked at the clock and saw it was two-thirty in the morning. She had been dreaming.

But it had seemed so real, and she thought that maybe if she was able to fall asleep again, she could get back to the images of the girl in the house. As she rolled over and stretched her arm, she touched something soft. Turning on her bedside lamp, she found the stuffed bear that was in her dream. Or at least it *seemed* like the same bear, because it didn't belong to Ravine. But it wasn't grey at all; it was brown.

Derek stood in a field watching two girls chase each other. One looked about sixteen years old, and the other six or so. They both had long, black hair and bright green eyes, and they were clearly related. Their clothes and their hair made them look like people in old photographs.

He wondered if they knew he was watching them.

The girls wore old-fashioned dresses that hung to the middle of their calves. He thought the dresses were grey, but he couldn't be sure because even the grass and the sky looked grey. There wasn't a hint of green or blue. Everything he could see was like a black-and-white photograph, except the bright green eyes of the two girls.

The older girl caught the younger one and lifted her high into the air, twirling her round and round until they both fell onto the grass, laughing. When they finally sat up, the older girl looked directly at Derek. She stared at him, and he knew she saw him. He tried to smile, to acknowledge her presence, but his whole body seemed to be paralyzed. Incapable of movement or speech, he was only able to watch.

The older girl helped the little one up, and they held hands while they danced around in a circle. It looked as if they were playing ring-around-the-rosy or a similar game. Derek noticed that the girls seemed to float instead of planting their feet on the ground. And even when they fell to the ground, their bodies seemed to hover slightly above the grass.

The older girl looked toward Derek again and held him in her gaze. He wondered if she was trying to tell him something.

She helped the younger girl up from the grass, and the two started to pick the forget-me-nots that were growing wild in the field. Once they had gathered a large bouquet, they slowly floated toward Derek. He watched as the figures came closer, amazed that he didn't feel afraid.

They stopped in front of him, holding out the flowers, and he held the gaze of the older girl. She seemed sad. He looked at the younger girl, who was holding the older girl's hand. His heart raced. He wondered if Ravine had seen her yet. He hoped not. Derek couldn't pry his eyes away from the little girl. She looked like Rachel.

When he reached out to take the flowers, the two girls vanished into thin air, leaving Derek with the sensation that he was falling, falling, falling.

Suddenly, he jerked awake.

It had all been a dream.

He blinked his eyes a couple of times, trying to adjust to the darkness of his room, and looked at his clock. Quarter past three. He stretched out his arms and touched something strange on his bed. Not sure what it was, he flicked on the bedside lamp and found fresh forget-me-nots neatly bunched on his bed.

Chapter Nine

Despite what she had promised herself, Ravine didn't sleep late Saturday morning. She awoke at eight o'clock. Well, maybe eight was sleeping in a little bit, since she had to be up by seven on school days. But for Ravine, sleeping in meant getting up just in time for lunch. It was almost a rule that she hadn't slept late enough unless her mother came into her room to open the blinds and complain that she was wasting the day.

But this Saturday morning was different; she was up and dressed and had already phoned Derek by ten past eight.

He answered the phone and, when he heard her voice on the line, he skipped hello and blurted out: "I had the weirdest dream last night!"

Derek explained his dream to Ravine, talking a mile a minute. He told her what he had found in his bed and kept skipping from thought to thought as he tried to tell her everything. It was all so real, he said. The older girl had looked right at him. He was sure they both knew he was there, and neither the girls nor he had been afraid.

When Derek finally paused long enough to take a breath, Ravine told him about her dream.

They agreed to meet at the house in half an hour, with the flowers and the teddy bear.

Ravine picked up the brown bear and held it close to her chest. It gave her a sense of closeness with the strange girl she had met in her sleep. Derek had described the older girl he saw, and he and Ravine were convinced that she was the same person in both dreams. They both figured she was probably a lot older than them, sixteen or so. And they were pretty sure she was Isabel. But they wondered who the little girl was.

Derek got dressed quickly, grabbed the now-wilted flowers and ran down the stairs, yelling to his mom that he was going over to see Ravine. Grace knew the kids would be spending most of the summer together; they always did. But she was surprised that her son was up and out so early this morning.

Ravine was already standing in front of the Morgans' house when Derek got there. Together, they examined the bear and the flowers.

"What do you think this means, Ravine? You're better than me at figuring out stuff like this."

"I think Isabel is trying to tell us not to be afraid of her," Ravine said.

Derek nodded.

Then they stepped onto the lawn at 56 Water Street and vanished.

As they walked up the rickety steps, they were surprised to see the front door open. They hesitated and peeked inside before stepping in. It didn't seem as dark as it had when they were last here, and they didn't think that was only because it was early in the day. The whole house seemed somehow brighter, less gloomy, and not quite so grey. They could see colours now, even if they were dull and faded.

Standing just inside, they paused to look around in the dim light. The peeling wallpaper was so badly faded that they couldn't make out what the pattern had been. The chandelier was covered in dirt, and long cobwebs trailed from it in stringy lines of silk. Crystal tear drops hung from the chandelier's fixtures, and the fuzzy light in the house glinted off them, as though time had completely failed to make them dull. Despite the dirt and the cobwebs, the great chandelier was still beautiful.

There was a red velvet Victorian couch and a chair that matched it. Much of the cloth was ripped off both pieces of furniture, and some of the cloth looked like it might have been touched by flames. The wood on the furniture was chipped and blackened.

"Do you smell that?" Ravine asked as they walked around the main floor of the house.

Derek twitched his nose and nodded. There was some kind of unpleasant odour, but it was not like anything he had ever smelled.

They entered the kitchen and found it was huge. It had a big wood-burning stove, a large, rectangular wooden table, and some scattered broken chairs. They were amazed by how many cupboards the kitchen had.

Derek started to ask where the refrigerator was but stopped, remembering they probably didn't have refrigerators so long ago. "Never mind," he said.

"The smell seems to be throughout the whole house," Ravine said. "I wonder why we never smelled it before. What is it?"

"Don't know. Maybe we were too busy being scared to notice any smells," Derek said.

They wandered around the first floor, brushing their hands gently over the furnishings and slowly absorbing the atmosphere of this place as they touched more of the Roberts' things. The wooden stair rail was hidden under a thick layer of dust, which felt soft under Ravine's fingers.

As they walked up the steep, narrow staircase, each rotting stair screeched beneath their feet, even though the steps seemed to be solid. The hall at the top of the stairs was also narrow, with two doors on either side.

The first door on their left was open, and they stood looking into a large room. At one time it must have been majestic.

"I guess this was her parents' bedroom," Derek said.

They stood for a few minutes looking inside. A stone fireplace occupied one corner, and one wall was dominated by floor-to-ceiling windows. About half the glass was now broken, and the tattered wallpaper showed a faded flowery pattern. The once-pristine red velvet drapes, now torn, swayed slightly as a soft summer breeze came through the open windows.

This room seemed bright and almost cheery because it was filled with sunlight, no longer blocked by the shredded drapery. The wooden floors had lost all their shine and were covered in a thick layer of dust. But Derek and Ravine could see the floorboards were once beautifully patterned hardwoods.

Suddenly, Ravine began to feel light-headed, and she started to sway; everything around her became dark.

She felt as if she had been taken back in time or was watching an old movie. She was looking at this same bright bedroom and could smell the light fragrance of a man's cologne mingled with the flowery scent of a woman's perfume. A tall, elegant woman stood before Ravine, the woman's dark chestnut hair wrapped in a bun and lustrous diamonds strung around her slender neck. Beside her stood a handsome man with hair that was almost black and a mustache that curled up at the ends. He was looking at his gold pocket watch. Where were they going? Ravine wondered. She guessed these were Isabel's parents; they looked like they were dressed for a fancy ball. She watched as the man walked over to his wife, put his arm around her bare shoulder, and led her out of the room.

Derek caught Ravine as she started to fall.

"Ravine! Are you okay?"

She could hear his voice but couldn't bring him into focus. He held her as he watched her eyelids flutter. When she opened her eyes, the ghosts from the past were gone, and she realized she was leaning against Derek.

She let go of him and nodded.

"They were here. Isabel's mother and father were here. They were standing right in front of me, as if I had been taken back in time. I saw them, Derek. I really did."

Derek rested his hand lightly on her shoulder and nodded. He believed her. Derek knew that Ravine sometimes saw things, and he trusted that she would tell him about them when she was ready.

But why was Isabel showing them her parents? What was she trying to tell them?

Derek and Ravine decided to move on and went to the bedroom opposite the one they had just come from. This must have been Isabel's room.

On the seat at the bay window were the remains of many stuffed animals. The once-fancy window curtain, like everything else in the house, was faded and ripped and had lost most of its frills. The decorative pillows on the seat no longer looked soft and comfy. The canopy had rotted over the bed, and Derek and Ravine could only guess that the wallpaper had once been pretty shades of pink.

But Ravine could imagine how beautiful the room must have looked, filled with frilly pink bedding and decorative lace and silk pillows.

The closet door was open, and Derek and Ravine could see several beautiful dresses still hanging in Isabel's closet. But the dresses, once genteel and fancy, were now dingy and hanging limp. Ravine touched one of the dresses and got a dusty, greasy film on her fingers. She put her hand up to her face to look more closely.

By now, the smell upstairs was overpowering, and Ravine started to choke. It was the same smell they had noticed throughout the house, but they still couldn't make out what it was. It was very pungent and smelled as though something was rotting; it was like a mixture of garbage, wet leaves, stinky sewer smell, and maybe smoke. But even that didn't really seem to describe it.

The smell seemed to be stronger here, and Ravine put her hand to her throat and began to cough. She quickly ran out of the room, gasping for air, with Derek running behind her yelling, "Are you okay? Are you okay? What's wrong, Ravine?"

In the hallway, Ravine was able to catch her breath, although the smell was still repulsive. Derek was relieved when she said she was feeling better.

"I think Isabel is communicating with me. I bet she is trying to tell me how she died," Ravine said in a shaky voice.

"How did she die? Do you know?" Derek asked as Ravine moved down the hall. The bathroom was the next room, and its door was open, so they continued to the last room and found the door closed.

"She must have choked to death. That is the only thing I can think of. I couldn't breathe in that bedroom, and I felt like I was choking on something. I'm sure Isabel is trying to show me what happened, to tell me how she died."

Ravine recognized this last door and tried the handle. "Something important is behind here, Derek. I don't know why Isabel won't let us in, but this was the door I saw in my dream. See? Here's the little ribbon that was tied around the handle. And it was locked in my dream, too. I'm positive Isabel is entering our thoughts while we sleep." A chill ran up her spine.

Seeing her shiver, Derek started to feel uneasy. "Where is Isabel anyway?" he asked, determined to retain his composure.

"Let's check the backyard," Ravine said. "It's the only place we haven't been yet."

Derek nodded. They retraced their steps down the narrow staircase and headed to the back door they had seen off the kitchen.

In the yard, Isabel was pushing a younger girl on a swing. Derek whispered that this was the same girl Isabel had shown him in his sleep. Except for the brilliant green of the two girls' eyes, everything in the yard was in shades of grey. The younger girl bore a striking resemblance to Isabel, like a miniature of the older girl. She also had long, dark hair with bangs that hung over her eyes, and she wore a long dress similar to Isabel's and lace-up shoes.

Derek glanced at Ravine. She was staring at the younger girl. Her eyes misted. Derek placed his hand on Ravine's shoulder. He knew what she was thinking. He had those same thoughts when he first saw the younger girl. Ravine turned toward Derek and forced out a smile, and he put his hands in his pockets.

The swing stopped, and Isabel lifted off the younger girl. She gave the girl a hug but when she did, the little girl vanished.

Suddenly, Ravine knew. Instinctively, she knew the younger girl was Isabel's sister, and it was her that Isabel had lost. It was this girl she was searching for. This must be Sarah.

Ravine knew the connection now, and she suddenly felt close to Isabel, closer than she had felt to anyone since Rachel died. She could feel Isabel's anguish as soon as the little girl disappeared. Sarah was her sister, and Isabel lost her; Ravine could share those feelings.

Isabel looked distraught and began floating around the yard, calling to the girl who had disappeared.

"Sarah," she cried. "Where are you?"

Derek and Ravine could hear her clearly now. Frantically, she searched, floating behind the trees and bushes. Then she moved past Derek and Ravine into the house, still calling for Sarah.

Ravine and Derek followed, trying to call to Isabel only to find their voices fading into nothing. They climbed the stairs after her in time to see her float through the locked door. Derek pushed against it as hard as he could, but it was no use; there was no way that door would budge unless Isabel allowed them to open it.

After waiting a while to see if Isabel would return, they tried the door one more time and then went downstairs. They figured they had probably seen the last of Isabel for today.

They left 56 Water Street and, as soon as they reached the pavement, Derek remarked how odd it was that no one ever seemed to see them come or go from the house; no one ever seemed to be looking when they disappeared or reappeared. He wondered if Isabel controlled that, too.

Sitting on the boulevard grass looking back at the house, they could faintly see a figure floating around in the locked bedroom.

"I think it's time to find out more about Isabel Roberts," Derek said.

Ravine agreed. "It's the only way to solve the mystery. It's the only way to free Isabel and send her home."

Derek looked at his watch. It was only nine o'clock. Time had stood still again.

"What do you want to do now?" Derek asked as he flicked a pebble onto the road.

Ravine shrugged. "I don't know. What do you want to do?"

The sun shone brightly, promising a hot and sunny day. Perfect for swimming.

Ravine really wanted to go back into the house but she figured Derek would rather spend the first day of summer vacation doing something a little more fun. But she didn't want to let go of Isabel Roberts yet. As she held the brown bear close, she got an idea.

"I say we check out the graveyard. Maybe we'll find out something there," Ravine said, looking at Derek.

"The graveyard? Why would we want to do that?" he said. Looking up at the clear sky, he continued, "Couldn't we do something normal? Like swimming or playing at the park? Do you know how far away the cemetery is?"

"Yes, I do. We'll have to ride our bikes and probably bring a lunch. We'll tell your mom we're going on a picnic. A picnic at Summerhill Cemetery! Oh, Derek, I'm pretty sure we will find some of the answers there."

The look on Derek's face said he had had enough of ghosts for one day. Ravine knew he wanted to help Isabel, but he didn't seem too thrilled about the graveyard.

"Why don't we just go swimming? It's too hot to be biking. Especially all the way to Summerhill," he said. "We can ride our bikes there another day when it's not so hot."

Ravine crossed her arms over her chest and scowled at him. "Don't you want to solve this mystery?"

Derek stared at Ravine. "This is a big deal to you, isn't it?"

"Yes."

Awkwardly, he put his arm around her shoulder. He had been at the hospital. He had been at the funeral. And he understood that helping Isabel would help Ravine find peace.

"This isn't going to bring back Rachel, you know," he said gently. It was the first time he had said her name out loud since the funeral.

Ravine looked up into his eyes. Derek was almost a whole head taller than her. He was also much bigger, and beside him, she looked like his younger sister.

Her voice was shaking. "What if she is out there searching for me?"

Derek shook his head. "She's not, Ravine. She knows where you are, and she knows how much you all loved her."

Ravine nodded. She knew Derek was right. But she needed to do this.

"Get your bike," he said, "and meet me at my house in fifteen minutes. I'll get my mom to pack us a lunch."

He watched as she ran across the street to her house.

He slowly walked to his own place, scuffing his shoes on the road and thinking about Rachel. The first day of summer vacation and a trip to the graveyard didn't seem to go together. He did want to help Isabel and to solve this mystery. But most of all, he wanted to help Ravine.

Derek opened the front door and called his mother. He kicked off his runners and headed into the kitchen, plopping himself into a chair. His mother was on the phone, and he waited for her to finish. He tapped his fingers impatiently on the table, and his mother glared at him in annoyance.

Just then, Ravine came in through the back door, letting it slam behind her. She sat down beside Derek and tapped her feet impatiently, waiting for Mrs. Radley to finish her conversation.

When she finally hung up the phone, it had barely touched the cradle when Derek blurted out, "Can you make us a picnic lunch?"

It took Ravine and Derek almost an hour to ride to the cemetery, even though they had ridden at a fast and steady pace. When they finally got there, Derek's legs felt wobbly. They were like rubber bands, or like a piece of gum that had been chewed too long. He had never ridden that far on his bike, and it was too hot for this today.

They chained their bikes to the wrought iron gate and walked up the steep hill, leaving their backpacks at the bottom. The only movement of the air seemed to be their own breathing.

It was almost three years ago that they had last been here. Derek remembered Ravine's mother being held up by her father as she cried uncontrollably. He recalled the crowd, all dressed in black, and the little stuffed bears placed on Rachel's grave. Eventually, the bears were donated to charity. But Ravine had kept one, which she kept hidden in the back of her closet. Derek knew that, and he was sure she hadn't told anyone else about it.

Ravine looked at Derek, and he could see the strength in her eyes. He could see that she was determined to find Sarah.

"This is a creepy place. Even in the daylight," Derek said. He took her hand, gave it a tight squeeze, and then dropped it quickly. He wanted to be strong for her. He wanted to be the brave one, but being around a whole lot of dead people was not his idea of a good time. And he was beginning to realize that Ravine had a solid strength in her.

"Yes, but it's quiet," Ravine tried to joke.

"Do you think the cemetery's in alphabetical order, like the phone book?" Derek asked.

Ravine shrugged. "I don't know, but I doubt it. People don't die in alphabetical order."

They looked at the hill full of graves spread out in front of them. Some of the gravestones were small crosses, and some had flowers planted around them. Some towered with importance, threatening to overpower the smaller flat plaques. Others had obviously not been tended for a long time and were leaning or had fallen over. Off to the side, there was one little area surrounded by an iron fence where the stones had six-pointed stars on them and some kind of writing that Ravine and Derek couldn't read.

They meandered slowly through the headstones, lost in the world of the dead. They read the inscriptions they could make out, but many were too faded from the effects of sun and rain. They tried to imagine worlds and lives for all these people who were buried and gone. Who were they, what did they do, where did they live, and how did they die? Derek and Ravine noticed headstones here and there for children who had only lived a few years. So many of these forgotten people never made it past the age of thirty. And there seemed to be a lot of them who died in 1918.

Most of the names meant nothing to them, but one caught their attention: Abigail Baldwin, 1872–1882. Ravine stopped at the headstone and ran her fingers across the dates, wondering what happened to this little girl. Abigail had died at the same age she and Derek were now. There was a family named Baldwin on the street next to Water Street, and Ravine wondered if this young girl might be related to them.

"Let's walk that way," Ravine said, pointing in the direction of a large tombstone with a cross.

"Okay," Derek agreed. Walking was helping him to get the feeling back in his legs. He started to think that maybe coming here today wasn't such a bad idea.

They continued wandering for a few minutes when Derek suddenly tripped and fell on his stomach. He landed on a gravestone that was lying flat and scraped his knee.

"Are you okay?" Ravine asked, bending down beside him. "Oh my gosh, you're bleeding!"

"It's just a little blood. I'll be okay," he said, standing up and examining his knee.

Ravine bent down and, without thinking, brushed the dirt off the gravestone. There was a bit of blood on the stone from Derek's knee.

"Look where you fell," she said. "Isabel Roberts, 1885–1901. Tripping here was no accident."

Just as she spoke, the wind picked up and howled in their ears. Ravine stood up, and the wind started to swirl rapidly, whipping her hair around her face.

"She's here," Ravine whispered.

Derek continued to wipe the dirt off the gravestones beside Isabel's. Ivan Roberts, 1853–1901, and Rose Roberts, 1866–1901.

"They all died in the same year," said Derek. "Do you think they all died at the same time? That seems pretty likely, eh? Some kind of accident maybe."

Ravine answered the questions with one of her own. "Where's Sarah? I don't see Sarah here anywhere. If she was Isabel's sister, she should be buried here. Even if she didn't die at the same time. Why isn't she here?"

"I don't know. Maybe she wasn't part of the family," Derek said, sounding uncertain. But they both knew that couldn't be right. The little girl looked so much like Isabel. The two girls had to have been sisters.

The wind continued to blow, and a soft voice whispered, "Find her. Please help me find her."

As the voice trailed away, they looked up to find Isabel floating around the cemetery and calling out Sarah's name. Then, as quickly as she had appeared, she vanished. When Isabel was gone, the wind slowed to a gentle breeze.

Derek and Ravine stood facing each other, convinced that the person Isabel was looking for was her little sister.

"She has to be," Ravine said. "They look so much alike. Who else could it be?"

Derek agreed; there was too much resemblance between the girls for them to be unrelated. But why wasn't Sarah here?

"Maybe she was Isabel's cousin?" Derek suggested.

Ravine shook her head. No. They were sisters. She recalled the feelings of anguish she sensed in Isabel when the younger girl disappeared from the backyard earlier. Where was Sarah? She guessed the little girl didn't die at the same time as the others, or she would be buried here, too. So when did she die?

What happened to Sarah Roberts?

Derek and Ravine decided the discovery of the gravestones was enough for one day. Before heading back down the hill, they visited one more grave. Ravine knelt in front of her sister's tombstone. "*Rachel Crawl*," it said. "*Dearly Beloved.*"

Rachel had died three years earlier, when she was only six years old. Although it had been a slow sickness, Rachel stayed happy through most of it. And that made it harder to let her go, because she always seemed so close to getting better.

Ravine knew it was too late now to say she was sorry for any bad times. So it was only the good times that she carried around in her heart.

She missed her sister.

Derek knelt down with Ravine, holding her hand and waiting while she quietly sobbed.

They stopped at the bottom of the hill to eat their lunch before beginning the long ride home. Ravine was sure that Isabel was still calling out for Sarah, although she appeared to have left the cemetery. Ravine could feel it in her heart, as if Isabel had temporarily taken part of Ravine into her or had put part of herself into Ravine. The thought of Isabel's ghost searching for Sarah all these years made Ravine very sad.

By the time they got back to Water Street, it was almost supper time. Ravine glanced at Derek's watch. She had exactly three minutes to get home. If she was even one minute past five, she would have to endure her mom's "responsibility" speech. Of all the routine lectures, that was the one she hated most, and she didn't need it today. She said good-bye to Derek and hurried home as fast as she could.

Derek coasted into his driveway and parked his bike on the lawn. He opened the door, calling out to his mom.

Grace appeared from the kitchen. "How was your picnic?" she asked.

"Great!" Derek said.

He walked into the living room, and his mom followed. He sat down on the couch beside Danielle, who was watching television. His mom kept staring at him.

"What?" he asked with some annoyance in his voice. His mom shook her head, frowning.

"What did I do?"

Danielle looked up, curious what this was about.

"Oh, Derek," his mom said. "Brand new pants! Brand new! And you've got dirt ground right into them. Did you think I wouldn't find them in the back of your closet? Honestly, Derek, every time I buy you something new, you wreck it in a day. Why do I bother?"

Derek sighed. He'd forgotten about his dirty pants.

"And now you've cut your knee," she said. She turned to leave, shaking her head, then added: "Well, at least you were wearing shorts this time."

Danielle smirked.

"I'm sorry, Mom, I really am," Derek said.

He was about to say that he could explain, but this time he couldn't. All he could do was give her a sheepish grin, the one that showed his dimples. The grin that usually got him out of trouble. Her face softened when she saw it, and she went back into the kitchen, mumbling to herself about boys and dirt.

Derek told Danielle to stop laughing, but she continued as she flipped through the channels.

"Go eat dirt!" she said.

As Derek walked upstairs to his room, he muttered nasty things about his sister under his breath and sat down in front of the keyboard. He typed in "*Eastern Times-News* Isabel Roberts." It was time to unravel the mystery of the dark-haired, green-eyed girl.

Chapter Ten

The house was quiet, and the only light came from the computer screen. Derek's mother and sister had gone to bed hours ago, and Derek continued to search for information online. Rubbing his tired eyes, he realized Madeline was right; this wasn't easy. Without an exact date, it was a lot of work to find out anything about Isabel Roberts.

A couple of hours earlier he had decided the only way to find any information on the Roberts family was to key in every date starting at the beginning of 1901. He had already guessed there must have been an accident or something that killed all three of them at once. And that probably meant there was a story in the newspaper.

His fingers were stiff, and his hands ached. But he couldn't give up now.

He was lucky that the full copy of every *Eastern Times-News* was archived online. But it wasn't indexed that far back, so he had to read every article in every daily paper. He had already searched to the end of May 1901.

Derek stood up and stretched his neck and his back. He hadn't realized just how sore his shoulders were, too. Most of his body ached from being bent over the computer for so many hours.

He walked to the window and gently pushed the curtain aside. The shadow of 56 Water Street was still clear in the pale moonlight, black and disturbing. The lights were flickering.

On. Off. Slow. Fast.

It was Isabel.

He sat back down at the computer. He would not give up. He started to punch in more dates, still coming up with nothing. He began to feel drowsy, and his head nodded, hitting his keyboard. All Derek could think about was sleep, but he had to keep on looking. Something was telling him the answer was here. Even if he wanted to give up now, he couldn't. For Isabel, and for Ravine, he knew he had to find out what happened to Sarah Roberts.

When he finally keyed in June 18, 1901, he woke from his drowsiness with a start. The front page carried a picture of 56 Water Street. Or what was left of it. The lead story was about the fire that had destroyed the house.

There was also a picture of the Roberts family; the caption said it was taken on September 2, 1900.

Derek switched on the printer and printed the whole newspaper in case there was more inside. And he made a hard copy of the next two weeks of papers as well. When he was done, he sat on his bed with the information he had gathered.

He looked out the window, watching the house for a couple of minutes. Then he started to read ...

Ravine had gone to bed early. Her legs were sore, and she was tired from the long bike ride.

Her mother was worried when she didn't come down for supper and went upstairs to check on her. Tapping on the door and getting no answer, she gently pushed it open. Ravine had fallen asleep in her clothes, on top of her bed.

Her mother walked over and opened the window to let in the night breeze and then covered Ravine with a light blanket. Kissing her on the forehead, she glanced toward the picture on the nightstand and held Rachel in her stare. If only there could be one more day with her.

She whispered her love to Ravine and then quietly shut the door behind her.

Ravine didn't stir. She was lost in a dream that Isabel had taken her into. She was watching a scene from Isabel's life, a picture that played itself out as if it were on a movie screen ...

Sarah came running into Isabel's room like she did every morning. She jumped on the bed and snuggled deep into the covers beside her big sister. Isabel put an arm around her and gave her a kiss.

"Do you know what day it is today?" Sarah asked.

"Is it Christmas?"

Sarah giggled. "Nooo, silly, guess again."

"Valentine's Day?"

"Nooo, it's not Valentine's Day," Sarah said. "Guess harder. It's a very important day."

Isabel hugged her little sister. She remembered the day Sarah was born as one of the happiest days of her life. Sarah was so small, and when her mother placed the baby in her arms, an instant bond formed.

No matter where Isabel went, Sarah wanted to go, too. Everything Isabel did, Sarah wanted to do. She was Isabel's shadow.

Isabel doted on Sarah. When her friends were fighting with their brothers and sisters, Isabel was playing with Sarah and teaching her how to do many things. Isabel was more patient than a teacher, more nurturing than most mothers, and more forgiving than most saints.

"If it is not Christmas and not Valentine's Day, but it is still a very important day, then it must be … it must be your birthday!" And she tickled Sarah's ribs.

Sarah jumped up and down on the bed. "Yes! It's my birthday!"

Isabel reached out and squeezed her close. She was as excited as Sarah. And she couldn't wait to give Sarah her present. She had spent an entire month designing and sewing a beautiful dress, and she was very pleased with the outcome. She had used expensive velvet in a deep shade of red with cream-coloured silk for the sash and collar. While Sarah slept, Isabel had spent many hours sewing layers of cotton crinoline with stitched roses.

Their mother bought Sarah a pair of shiny black shoes and a dainty little pearl necklace to match the dress.

Their father had a surprise, too. Tonight, the entire family was going to dine at a fancy restaurant and then going to an opera. Sarah's first opera!

"Did Momma make me a cake?" Sarah asked.

"Now, if I told you that, it would not be a surprise," said Isabel with a twinkle in her eye.

The girls got out of bed when they heard their father shut the door to the bathroom.

Isabel took Sarah's hand. "Now try not to be too loud this morning. Papa must be tired. He worked late last night."

Sarah nodded.

When they got to the kitchen, they found their mother had decorated the room with pink and purple ribbons.

"Good morning, princess!" their mother exclaimed, holding a cake in her hands. It had six candles, and they were already lit. Sarah clapped her hands together in delight.

"Ohhh, birthday cake for breakfast! What a wonderful idea," Isabel said.

The Roberts family sat down and had cake for breakfast. Sarah opened her gifts, and when she lifted out the dress from Isabel, her green eyes opened wide. She ran to Isabel and gave her a hug that almost choked her.

Sarah wanted to wear the new dress right away, but her mother insisted that she wait until they were ready to go out for dinner. After only a little bit of pouting, Sarah brightened because Isabel said she would take her outside and push her on the swing.

"Now that I'm six years old, I'll be able to go to school with you in the fall," Sarah said. "Won't that be lots of fun, Isabel?"

Isabel pushed her higher, and Sarah squealed with laughter.

"It certainly will be. We can walk to the schoolhouse together and walk home together, and I can help you with your homework. But I cannot sit with you in class because Miss Hardy puts all the small children in the front and all the older children in the back."

"That's okay; at least we can play together at recess," Sarah said.

"Yes, we can do that."

They spent the morning picking flowers and reading stories. As usual, they helped their mother hang the clean laundry on the line to dry. Sarah gave Isabel the pins, and Isabel hung the clothes.

It was a wonderfully warm day, and the anticipation of an evening at the opera kept building as the day went on. It wasn't long before their mother called the girls to get ready for their big outing.

Isabel went to her bedroom and chose her favorite yellow dress. She was sitting in front of the mirror, combing her long, dark hair and humming to herself, when Sarah appeared at the doorway.

"What do you think?" Sarah asked, twirling around in her new red velvet dress.

Isabel was delighted; the dress fit perfectly, and Sarah was truly a little princess. Mother had done her hair up with a silk rose, leaving strands of curls to frame her tiny, round face.

"You look lovely," Isabel said. "You will be the prettiest girl at the opera."

Sarah smiled, then left, closing the door behind her.

Isabel continued to brush her hair while she daydreamed about Jordan. He would be at the opera tonight, and she wanted to look her best. Her friends all said that he liked her. Maybe he would come over and talk to her tonight.

The Roberts family sat quietly watching *The Magic Flute*. The lively music swirled, and the performers kept the audience entranced.

During the opera, Sarah kept a close eye on her sister so she would know what to do. If Isabel laughed, Sarah laughed. When Isabel applauded, Sarah applauded. At one point, Isabel smiled and reached for Sarah's hand, holding it in her lap for the remainder of the show.

Bravo! Bravo! The audience stood as the performers took their curtain calls. Isabel waved her hanky and clapped. Sarah did the same.

Then it was over, and the audience began to file out. Many people gathered in the pleasant evening air, chatting about the opera while they awaited their carriage rides.

"It was a good performance," Jordan said, coming up behind Isabel and touching her on the shoulder. She turned around gracefully and gave him a shy but friendly smile.

"It certainly was. This is my favorite opera," she said with a little more confidence.

"Mine, too," Jordan said. "Mozart is wonderful."

Sarah grabbed Isabel's hand and listened while her sister spoke to her friend. She didn't want to interrupt; she had a feeling Isabel really liked this boy.

It was late when the Roberts family got home. Isabel climbed into bed, thinking about Jordan. "I am going to marry him someday," she said to herself as she closed her eyes.

Sarah had fallen asleep in the carriage on the way home and had to be carried to bed, still asleep.

"Goodnight, my princess. Have wonderful dreams," her mother whispered as she closed the door to Sarah's room behind her.

Hours later, when the darkness was deep and still, a killer silently moved through the house. There was no warning of his arrival, and with terrible speed he tore through the house, leaving nothing but ashes and ruin.

Derek crawled into bed and hid under the sheets with the newspaper stories he had printed. He turned on the flashlight and stared at the headline: "Tragedy Strikes Water Street." Then he read:

> A devastating shock occurred when an early morning fire tore through the home of Ivan Roberts at 56 Water Street leaving him; his wife, Rose; and daughter, Isabel, dead. At three in the morning, the fire brigade was called out only to find the house engulfed in flames. They entered the building

and discovered the three bodies but were unable to put out the fire before much of the house was destroyed.

Authorities are still looking into the cause of the fire, but at this time no information will be released.

Ivan Roberts arrived from Russia eighteen years ago and became a successful wholesaler of fabrics and linens. He was known for his work with the poor, and he gave generously to the churches where he and his family volunteered to help feed unfortunates.

Neighbours said he was a truly outstanding member of the community. He and his family will be greatly missed.

Derek read another story, "Little Girl's Fate Uncertain":

What happens now to little Sarah Roberts, the only survivor of last weekend's tragic fire at 56 Water Street? With her family gone, the little girl is alone in the world, and her future looks bleak. After spending three days in the hospital, where she was treated for smoke inhalation, she has refused to speak. Staff at Memorial Hospital say that when she is sleeping, she calls out for her sister, Isabel. But she doesn't utter a word when she's awake.

Then, a week later: "Three Boys Charged in Tragic Fire."

Three boys have been charged with arson in the fire at 56 Water Street that claimed three members of the Roberts family in the early hours of June 18. Names have not been released, but the prosecutor has said he will ask for the maximum penalty.

The lads had been playing with homemade smoke pots when one of them thought he heard someone approaching. At that late hour, they thought it might be a patrolling policeman. Afraid of being caught, they ran to the back of the Roberts home and deliberately threw the burning pots through an open window, igniting the blaze.

Derek put down the articles. He hadn't noticed he had been crying until a tear fell onto the paper. As he turned off the flashlight and crawled out from under the covers, the wind suddenly blew through his window, sending his curtains into a state of panic. He looked up and, standing at the end of his bed was Isabel, floating slightly above the floor.

"Are you crying for me?" she asked softly.

He nodded and wondered if he was dreaming.

"Do not cry for me," Isabel said. "Just help me find Sarah." She floated back and forth through the room as though she was pacing. "Where is she? Where could my little sister be?"

Derek watched Isabel pace. Back and forth, she floated in front of him. He wished he could tell her what had happened to her little sister, but he still didn't know. The question Isabel was asking was the same one he was asking. Where was Sarah?

Derek started to speak but just as he was about to say something, the bedroom door swung open, and Isabel disappeared.

"Derek, it's three o'clock in the morning! Go to sleep," his mother said.

The following morning, Ravine lay in bed for a long time, staring at the ceiling and thinking about the scenes she had witnessed from Isabel's life. It seemed so real, and she knew Isabel was showing her these pictures for a reason.

Derek was going out of town with his mother and sister today to visit his grandmother, and Ravine wondered if she should go into the house by herself. She knew now that Isabel didn't want to hurt them, so there was nothing to fear.

She stretched her arms over her head and slowly crawled out of bed. Digging through the bottom drawer of her dresser, she found her favorite cut-off jeans and her old baseball shirt, the pink one with the rip on the left sleeve. The only girlish thing about Ravine was her favorite colour: pink.

She headed downstairs to the kitchen and could hear her parents' voices from the top step. They usually spent Sunday mornings at the kitchen table reading Saturday's news. They were most interested in the stock market reports, and they could sit and talk about them for hours.

"Good morning, Ravine," her father said, his nose stuck between the business pages.

Ravine sat down and helped herself to a piece of toast from the plate in the middle of the table.

"Here, sweetheart, have some eggs." Her mother passed her the bowl.

Ravine turned up her nose. Scrambled eggs were fine once in a while but after eating them every Sunday morning for the past ten years, they were starting to gross her out.

"Uh, no thanks, Mom. I'm not that hungry."

Her mother shrugged. "Want some more, Robby?"

Ravine picked at her toast. She plastered it with peanut butter just so she could lick it off while she listened to her parents talk about stocks and work and other boring stuff. She wished she could tell them everything that had happened to her and Derek the last two days. She imagined how a conversation like that would go.

"So anyway, Mom, while you and Dad spent a couple of boring days at work, Derek and I met a psychic. She is the most awesome person I have ever met. Then, Derek and I spent a day in the invisible house across the street. You know, the one you can't see. Oh, yes, and we rode our bikes to the graveyard to find out more information about the ghost that lives in the invisible house. You know, the one you can't see. And by the way, we also met the ghost, and she seems really nice."

Guess not, Ravine thought. Weird things are happening to me and Derek, but this was way beyond her parents.

Ravine left the crusts on her plate and listened to her parents quietly. If only she could tell her parents about the house and the ghost, maybe she wouldn't feel light years apart from them. Maybe they would have something to talk about that interested all three of them. Maybe it would make them a normal family again. Not that there was anything normal about seeing ghosts.

Ravine got up and placed her plate in the sink with the crusts still on it.

"I'm going to walk over to Joannie's to see if she wants to hang out."

"Where's Derek today?" her father asked, looking up from the paper.

"He has to go visit his grandma. I probably won't see him until tomorrow."

Once outside, Ravine walked straight across the street and stepped onto the lawn and disappeared.

She walked up to the front door and gently pushed it open. Standing in the doorway for a couple of seconds, she let her eyes get accustomed to the gloom before heading upstairs to Isabel's room. The closer she got, the harder it was to breathe. She was getting dizzy and, as she stumbled into Isabel's room, she tried to shut the door with her foot. But the room was spinning, and it was a struggle to keep her balance. Clutching at her throat, she lurched toward Isabel's bed and, with one last gulp of air, fell onto the bed and into total darkness.

Although it seemed like a much longer time, Ravine began to breathe easier after a few seconds; a couple of minutes later, the spinning finally stopped. Then, when she was sure everything was okay, she opened her eyes and immediately jumped off the bed, terrified.

All around her, flames licked at the walls and lunged toward her feet. She was surrounded, and the flames were between her and the door. Looking across the room, she could see Isabel's shadowy figure calling out words she could not quite hear.

Frantically, Ravine yelled to her, but Isabel didn't seem to hear or see her. Ravine screamed louder as the flames came closer. Just when the fire was about to swallow her, Ravine's legs crumbled beneath her, and she fell once again into complete darkness.

When Ravine finally opened her eyes, she was alone in the room. The flames were gone, and she was able to breathe. But she knew now what the smell was that she and Derek had not been able to identify: It was the smell of charred furniture and clothing, the smell of death.

Ravine wasn't sure how long she had been lying there, but when she stood up, she noticed a small burn mark on her arm. She shuddered and backed out of Isabel's room.

"You died in a fire, didn't you, Isabel?" she asked out loud, looking around. She waited for Isabel to appear, but there was no sign of her.

Ravine walked down the hall and leaned against the locked door. She turned the knob and, to her surprise, the door swung open easily. Almost afraid of what she might see, she hesitated. As she peeked through the crack, there was Isabel, sitting cross-legged and floating slightly above a bed. Ravine opened the door all the way.

It was a little girl's room. Ravine walked toward the dresser and picked up a picture of Isabel and Sarah in fancy dresses. Seeing the picture of Sarah this close, Ravine realized how much Isabel's sister resembled her own. Sarah's hair was the same colour as Rachel's. Her face was plump, and tiny freckles were sprinkled across her nose. Ravine shuddered. It was as if she were looking at a photo of Rachel, taken way back in time—a version of her sister from days gone by.

With the photo in her hand, she turned toward Isabel.

"She's your sister," Ravine whispered.

Isabel nodded.

But why couldn't they find Sarah's tombstone today? What happened to Sarah?

"You have been searching all these years for your sister, haven't you? Since the fire."

Isabel nodded. Ravine knew that Isabel could never rest until the mystery of her sister was solved.

"We'll find her, Isabel. I promise, we will."

She glanced up and looked into the mirror over the dresser, but Isabel seemed to be gone. Ravine turned around to find Isabel still floating slightly above the bed. Isabel made no reflection in the mirror, but this didn't surprise Ravine. She reached out with her hand, but that made Isabel suddenly vanish. The only sign left to show she had been there was a small damp spot on the bedspread where the girl's tears had fallen.

Ravine walked home. A hundred years was a long time to be searching for someone. She opened the front door and headed back to the kitchen.

"Wasn't Joannie home?" her mother asked.

Ravine sat down beside her dad, who was still flipping through the paper.

"Pardon?" Ravine asked.

"Joannie. You said you were going to Joannie's, but you're home again," her mother said.

"No, she wasn't home."

Ravine had forgotten that time stood still when they went into the house of Isabel Roberts.

Chapter Eleven

Ravine tossed in her sleep most of the night. Her mind was filled with the sights and sounds of Isabel's life. And, as she slept, Isabel again took Ravine into the world of a hundred years ago.

Isabel thought it was a lot later than it really was, but Miss Hardy finally dismissed her pupils. The last subject of the day was science, Isabel's least favorite class, and this day seemed to have dragged on a long time.

She gathered her books and ran down the steps of the small schoolhouse.

"Wait for me. I'll walk with you," Nancy called out to her.

Isabel turned to look over her shoulder. "Okay, but hurry. I need to rush home today," she said, slowing down so her friend could catch up.

"Why?" Nancy asked as she walked up beside her.

"My mother and father are going to a meeting at the town hall, and I have to look after Sarah."

"Don't you get tired of always looking after her? Wouldn't you prefer to go out with your friends instead of being stuck at home all the time?"

Isabel was Nancy's best friend. She liked Isabel's little sister, but she thought that Isabel missed out on a lot of fun because she was always babysitting.

"Oh, not at all," Isabel said. "I always enjoy spending time with her. She is such a good child."

The girls fell into stride with one another as they walked home.

"Where were you at recess?" Isabel asked.

Nancy grinned mischievously. "I was with Jeffrey," she announced.

Isabel stopped abruptly and turned to look at Nancy.

"You were not!"

Nancy saw the horrified look on Isabel's face, and she giggled.

"Oh, but I was. And you know what ...?"

"What?" Isabel asked.

"He's a great kisser."

"You did not!"

Isabel was horrified that Nancy would even consider joking about such a thing. Nancy would get into so much trouble if she was ever caught kissing a boy! Isabel shook her head and continued walking. How could Nancy do these things? Why did she always flirt with danger?

"Aren't you going to say anything?" Nancy asked.

Isabel continued to walk in silence.

"You're not mad, are you?" Nancy asked.

Isabel stopped. "Of course I am not mad. I am just concerned that one day you are going to get into a lot of trouble, that is all."

They walked the rest of the way home in silence. When they reached Isabel's house, she ran up the steps to the front door, leaving Nancy standing by herself. She turned around and waved. "I will see you tomorrow at school," Isabel called.

Nancy saw Sarah standing inside the door. Isabel put her book bag down and lifted her sister up in a hug.

Nancy watched until Isabel shut the door behind her. A part of her was jealous that Isabel always seemed so happy.

She thought about what Isabel had said and wondered why she did always have to sneak around, doing things that could get her into serious trouble. She didn't wonder about it too long, though, and went skipping down the path, thinking about the chores she had to do when she got home and whether she could avoid doing them.

Nancy was almost an exact opposite of Isabel, and people wondered how the two girls could be such close friends. But it was rare that anyone would talk about one of them without mentioning the other.

Ravine turned over in her sleep as Isabel walked her through some of the good times of her life. But the dreams quickly turned to sorrow.

Isabel floated as firemen fought their way through the flames. Sarah's screams filled the house but no one was alive to hear her panicked cries, except the firemen.

Isabel floated through the house desperately looking for Sarah. The air was thick, but for some reason she could not feel the heat from the fire, and she wasn't choking on the smoke.

She floated around the house calling out to Sarah, trying to get the attention of one fireman, but he ignored her. She followed him to the front and, when she looked down at the lawn, she saw three bodies.

Her mother. Her father. And herself.

Confused, she knelt beside her own body and, as she did, she heard the fireman saying to his captain that they had come too late. They placed sheets over the three bodies and waited for the coroner's wagon to arrive.

Shocked by what she saw, Isabel stood frozen. She was dead. She didn't know what being dead should be like, but she didn't feel dead. This wasn't what she expected. There on the ground, though, was her lifeless body. She bent over the bodies of her mother and father, crying, until she heard the soft sweet sound of her mother's voice coming from above her.

"Isabel, follow the light," the voice said.

She looked up. Above her, a bright light shone, blinding her view of the world she knew. Unable to control what was happening, she felt herself being pulled toward the warm, safe glow. The closer she got to her mother and father, the more she felt like she was being pulled home.

But just as she was about to reach the ray of light where her mother stood with outstretched arms, she heard a fireman yell: "There is a young child still alive in there!"

Frantically, the firemen raced inside, trying to locate Sarah by the sound of her cries. The roar of the flames had obscured her voice until now.

Isabel immediately turned away from the light. Using all the strength she could muster, she pulled away from the welcoming glow of the light and hurried back into the burning house to find her sister. But the smoke was too thick. By the time she reached the front staircase, two firemen rushed past her carrying a small body. Before Isabel had time to think about what to do next, she was standing alone, and the ambulance wagon was rushing to the hospital, taking Sarah away from her.

Isabel turned back to the light, where her mother had been, but it too had vanished. Isabel stood alone, in silence. Everything she had ever known and loved was gone. Vanished within just a few minutes.

Derek crawled into bed late. It had been a boring day sitting around his grandmother's coffee table playing checkers. He loathed checkers, but no one else in his family knew how to play chess.

He wondered what Ravine had been doing today. He wanted to show her the newspaper articles he had found about the Roberts family, but it was too late. Unfortunately, that would have to wait until tomorrow.

Derek closed his eyes and fell quickly into a sound sleep. But beneath his eyelids, the world of Isabel Roberts came to life, and he found himself sitting in the shadows, watching the dark-haired, green-eyed girl and a friend, as if they were close enough to touch.

"He loves me. He loves me not. He loves me!"

Isabel ripped off the last petal from the daisy. She was lying on her back under the big weeping willow tree in the front yard. Her friend Nancy was sitting beside her with her back against the trunk.

"Of course he loves you. Everyone knows that!" said Nancy.

Jordan and Isabel were going to get married. Everyone knew it. And everyone was pleased about it. Two special people and two prosperous and decent families would be joined together. It was right and proper. It was destiny.

"Who do you love?" Isabel asked.

"Nobody," said Nancy.

"What do you mean nobody? What about Jeffrey?"

"I don't love Jeffrey."

"But you kissed him," Isabel said, shocked.

"It was just a kiss. I wanted to see what it was like."

"Well, you have to love somebody," Isabel said. "How sad and lonely life would be if you did not love anybody."

"I'm telling you the truth. I'm going to get a job and go off to see the world. I love nobody, and I'm never getting married. I don't want to have kids, either," Nancy said.

"Do not be ridiculous, Nancy. Every girl wants to find her true love and get married and have children. Stop talking such nonsense."

Isabel didn't like it when Nancy talked that way. She couldn't even imagine what a lonely life Nancy would have if she actually did the things she talked about.

"Oh, Isabel, you live in a world of fancy. Life isn't really like that."

"Of course it is," Isabel said. "You will see."

The girls lay on the grass, quietly lost in their own daydreams, and Derek felt a sense of peacefulness come over him. Isabel's gentle personality seemed to enter his mind, allowing him to feel her emotions. He could feel she was a happy girl, content with growing up and marrying this young man, Jordan.

She was satisfied with the simple pleasures life offered and was able to create her own magic from small things. The dew sparkling like a string of pearls on the early morning flowers, the raindrops glistening and dancing in mid-afternoon summer showers, the colourful rainbows that graced the sky after the darkness of thunderstorms, the beauty of gentle snowflakes—all were small miracles to her. The little beauties of everyday life were all Isabel needed for a light heart.

Then, before Derek's eyes, the sky quickly darkened, and the wind swirled dirt in the air. He closed his eyes as dust scurried everywhere. In his own darkness, he could hear screams of terror. He wanted to open his eyes, but he was afraid. His skin felt cold, and his head ached. Then, as quickly as the wind stormed in, it stopped.

When Derek finally opened his eyes, he was no longer outside Isabel's house. He was inside, and the ghost of Isabel lay on the floor with her hair sprawled out around her. She was motionless. He approached her quietly but she did not move.

When he noticed her shoulders shaking, he sat on the floor beside her in the soot and ashes. She looked up into his eyes, and he noticed the colour of her eyes had faded into the same shade of grey as everything else.

"They took her away. I cannot find her ..."

With those words, Isabel vanished.

Chapter Twelve

Derek and Ravine sat in a quiet corner of the library. The original newspapers from a hundred years earlier were too old to still be around, but they had been faithfully reproduced in large books. The kids were surrounded by a pile of these books and had carefully gone through them, page by page, until they finally found the right time period.

The records Derek had found on the Internet gave them the right time frame and lots of information. But they knew it would be easier to search this way, so they wouldn't miss anything. They still had not been able to locate much more about Sarah.

After reading many articles about the fire that killed Isabel and her parents, they knew for sure that Sarah had survived; Isabel wasn't mistaken about that. So what happened to the little girl? Where did she go? Who did she live with? They knew she had to be dead by now, but they could not find any obituary listing for her. And they knew hunting for a death notice might be a fruitless task because she could have lived to an old age, which would make it a very long search. Or she might have moved away and died somewhere else.

Ravine came across a small headline on the last page of a newspaper that was printed exactly one month after the fire.

"Look at this," she said. Pointing to the headline, she read in a hushed tone:

> It has been confirmed that Sarah Roberts has no living relatives in Canada. She has been placed in an orphanage for adoption. The girl hasn't spoken since the night of the fire when she lost her whole family.

Ravine stopped. Derek took the volume from her and read it again to himself.

"Obviously the hype had died down and people were already forgetting about the fire and going on with their lives," he said. "That's what happens.

Something tragic occurs and the newspapers are all over it until something bigger comes along and people's attention turns there. Look at the big headline here."

He pointed to the top of the front page and read out loud: "Man Killed When His Horse Gets Spooked."

Ravine read it with him.

"I guess that was more interesting than a fire that killed three people a month earlier," she added.

"Exactly," Derek said.

"Does it give the name of the orphanage she was placed in?" Ravine asked.

Derek continued reading from where Ravine had left off.

"Yeah, the Sisters of Prayer," he said.

"I've never heard of it. Maybe the librarian knows."

They knew they weren't going to find anything else here, so they closed the books and took them back to the newspaper desk. Derek had his notebook with all his notes under his arm.

Mrs. Hill, the librarian, was an older lady, older than Ravine's parents. They thought she might be older than Derek's grandmother, too. Ravine guessed she was old enough to have known people who were around at the time of the fire. If anybody knew anything about the Roberts family, it should be her. She might even have known Sarah.

Ravine handed the newspaper books back to Mrs. Hill and asked, "Have you ever heard about the Sisters of Prayer?"

Mrs. Hill took off her glasses. She looked younger without them balancing on the tip of her nose. But not much younger.

"The Sisters of Prayer," she said. "Why do you ask about them?" She put her elbows on the desk and leaned forward to look at the two children.

Derek glanced at Ravine and let her handle the explanation.

"Well, we came across a fascinating article about a little girl named Sarah Roberts, and it said she was placed in an orphanage called the Sisters of Prayer. We were wondering if it is still around."

The librarian looked surprised. "My, my, I haven't heard that name for a very long time. Sarah Roberts. What a tragic story."

Derek and Ravine looked at each other and waited for Mrs. Hill to continue.

"The Sisters of Prayer was an orphanage when Sarah was a child," the librarian said. "That's where she went to live after the tragedy. Later, it was made into a convent, and it is still there today."

"The one downtown beside the big church?" Derek asked.

Mrs. Hill nodded.

"Would they still have records on Sarah Roberts?" Ravine asked.

"Oh, I'm pretty sure they would. Even if they don't, someone there will surely know what happened to her."

The children thanked Mrs. Hill and opened the door, letting a bit of the hot, humid air into the coolness of the library.

"I think it's time we paid a visit to the convent," Ravine said, wiping the fog from her glasses. The temperature and humidity inside the library was so much lower than outside.

"Yeah, I think you're right," Derek said.

The convent was located downtown, so they decided to walk home first and get their bikes.

As she watched the children leave, Mrs. Hill smiled. She remembered her grandmother telling her tales about the Roberts family. Nana would always gaze far off into the distance with a sad look on her face when she told how her best friend died so suddenly in a house fire. She always got tears in her eyes when she told that story.

Mrs. Hill had pictures of her grandmother as a young girl, and Nana's best friend, Isabel, was in some of them. "Remembering the happy times keeps Isabel alive," her grandmother used to say, so she would tell stories about the two of them in their younger days.

Nana often said, "I lived her life. To keep her alive, I lived her dream for her."

When Mrs. Hill was little, she and Nana would go to Isabel's grave quite often. Sometimes they would plant forget-me-nots. Mrs. Hill hadn't been there since her grandmother passed away, and that was many years ago.

Now, these two bright-eyed children had brought up a name that Mrs. Hill had not heard for many years. As she reminisced, she realized someone else was standing at her desk, patiently waiting to ask a question. She put her glasses back on and asked how she could help.

They stood in front of the convent, intimidated by the large iron gates. Although they had passed this place many times, neither of them had ever been inside the convent walls. They had barely noticed it was there, let alone wonder about what happened inside.

"Do you think we are welcome here?" Derek asked, nervously.

"Of course we are. Everyone is welcome in the house of God," Ravine said. She looked around but was unable to find the latch to let them in.

"Maybe there's a doorbell somewhere," Derek said, trying to find one.

When neither of them could find a doorbell, Ravine started rattling a stick across the gates, making a tremendous amount of noise.

"What are you doing?" Derek whispered loudly, scared she was going to get them into trouble.

"I'm trying to get somebody's attention," she said, and continued the rattling.

Derek grabbed her arm in frustration to stop her from making so much noise.

"Everyone might be welcome in God's house, but I don't think he would appreciate you trying to break down his front door."

Ravine stopped and crossed her arms over her chest. She was about to say something rude to Derek when a dark figure appeared.

"Children, children, what is all this racket?" the figure asked in a soft voice.

It was a nun, dressed in black from head to toe. A large silver cross hung around her neck. Although they couldn't see much of her, her kindly face was lit with a smile that seemed pure and golden. But it was hard to determine if she was young or old, or something in between.

"We were wondering if you could let us in?" Derek asked, without giving a reason for their visit.

"Why, yes. I'll let you in. But if you should happen to come again, why don't you just use the doorbell on the wall over there?" The nun pointed to the ivy-covered wall. Behind the green vines, a gold buzzer peeked through. They both grinned and shrugged, feeling a little foolish.

"My name is Sister Catherine," she said, as she opened the gate for them. She spoke with a slight accent.

Without asking their names or the reason for their visit, she led them to the back of the main building and into a beautiful garden. There, she sat on a bench and invited them to sit with her.

Derek and Ravine sat on either side of Sister Catherine, looking at the flowers and shrubs. Rose bushes climbed over the brick wall surrounding the convent, and a small waterfall gurgled amongst the flower beds. A stone statue of Saint Francis stood beside the waterfall. The saint held a little nest in his hand, presently occupied by a small sparrow preening itself in the sun.

As if this was another world, Ravine felt far away from the busy city outside the convent. She couldn't hear any noise coming from the street, and she felt at peace.

"Now, tell me why two young children want to spend time at a convent instead of going to the beach or the park?" It was unusual for children to come calling, especially during summer vacation.

Ravine started.

"My name is Ravine Crawl, and this is my best friend, Derek Radley." She paused, unsure what to say next, and she looked to Derek for help.

Derek dug out the newspaper articles they had photocopied and simply handed them to Sister Catherine.

"My, my," said the nun. She was quiet for a few minutes as she read the articles.

Derek sat up taller as he and Ravine watched Sister Catherine. She seemed interested in what she read, and Derek hoped she might have some answers for them. This didn't seem to be new to her, rather a reminder of something she already knew about.

When the sister had finished, she handed the articles back to Derek and stared into the garden before she finally spoke.

"Sarah Roberts. No one has asked about her in a very long time."

"Did you know her?" Derek asked.

"Oh, heavens no, child! I wasn't born when that happened. That was a very long time ago. But everyone here knows about Sarah Roberts."

"You are so embarrassing," Ravine said, punching Derek in the arm. "Of course she didn't know her. What do you think she is, a hundred years old or something?"

Ravine shook her head as Derek gave her a dirty look.

Sister Catherine paused and stared into the distance again. It looked to Ravine as if the nun was wandering in her memories, even though she could not possibly have known Sarah.

"We live across the street from where Sarah Roberts used to live," Derek said, hoping to give a better explanation of why they were here.

"And so you are curious about the little girl who survived the fire," said Sister Catherine. "Everyone here will be pleased to know that Sarah's story has not been completely forgotten in the world outside these walls. All these years later, two bright, young children have found an article about her and want to know about her, about her life after the terrible fire."

Derek and Ravine both nodded.

Sister Catherine looked at Derek with a smile, and then at Ravine. She stood and said, "Follow me, please."

She led them around the brick walls, past all the pretty gardens, and into the convent's main building. Walking past the chapel and down a dark hall, Sister Catherine finally stopped in front of a closed room. She lifted an old-fashioned key from its peg by the door and fitted it into the lock. As the door opened, she turned on a dim light, revealing a small, sparsely decorated bedroom.

Derek and Ravine stood in the doorway. They didn't need Sister Catherine to tell them this was Sarah's room. They already knew.

A dusty photo of Sarah and Isabel sat on a tiny dresser. Placed carefully on the bed were a beautiful gold cross and a brown teddy bear. Ravine walked to the bed and picked up the bear. Startled, she thought it was the stuffed bear from her dream. But she shook her head, knowing she had left that bear on her own pillow that morning.

Sister Catherine sat on the bed with Derek and Ravine as they waited for the story of Sarah Roberts to unfold.

"A year after Sarah came to the Sisters of Prayer, the orphanage became a convent. The children who hadn't been taken into good homes were placed with foster families until adoptions could be arranged. All except for little Sarah Roberts," she said.

"But why?" Ravine asked.

"Sarah would not speak after the death of her family. So many doctors tried to help her, but Sarah had crawled deep inside herself and would not open up to anyone. So it was very difficult to find a family that wanted to care for her. The Sisters took pity and decided to care for her themselves; they raised her like she was their own. They loved her. Even though she never spoke, she was such a sweet and kind child. She never said another word after the fire, except sometimes in her sleep when she would call out her sister's name."

"But where did she go after that," asked Derek. "When she grew up. Did she get married? What happened to her?"

Sister Catherine stood. "Come with me again."

She shut off the light and, closing the door behind her, she took out the big key to lock away the tiny world of Sarah Roberts once again. The kids followed her back down the hallway.

She took them outside again, around the gardens, and into a small cemetery. They stopped at a gravestone set some distance from all the others.

They looked down and read out loud together: "*Sarah Roberts, 1895–1904.*"

"What happened to her?" Derek asked.

Ravine knelt down and picked a couple of the forget-me-nots planted beside the headstone.

"She died three years after she came here from complications of pneumonia," Sister Catherine said.

"Why wasn't she buried with her family?" Ravine asked.

"I'm not sure. But I guess the nuns considered her part of their family by then, so she was buried here."

It was all starting to make sense now, Ravine thought to herself. Isabel didn't know where to look for her sister, alive or dead.

"Do you know anything about Isabel Roberts?" Ravine blurted out.

Sister Catherine shook her head. "No, nothing. But if you are interested in Isabel Roberts, you might want to ask Mrs. Hill, the librarian. She has an interesting connection to that family."

It was seven o'clock when Derek and Ravine stood at the front door, ringing Mrs. Hill's bell. It took her a couple of minutes to answer. But, when she did, she smiled.

"I thought I might be seeing more of you two," she said, peering over the rims of her glasses and inviting them inside.

They followed Mrs. Hill into her living room, and she motioned for them to sit down.

"I suppose you want to hear more about Isabel Roberts," she said.

They nodded.

Reaching to the top of a bookshelf, she brought down a black photo album. Sitting between the two kids, she opened the book.

"My grandmother's name was Nancy," she began, turning to a picture of her grandmother when she was sixteen years old.

"She was known as a troublemaker, a rule breaker, a big dreamer," Mrs. Hill said. "She wanted a different life than most girls her age. She wanted to see the world, travel the seven seas, and fly to the moon. Those were her exact words."

Ravine laughed at that, eager to hear more.

"Those ambitions were not at all common for a young girl back then. People would have thought of her as a rebel, a wild child; she didn't have the everyday dream of meeting her handsome prince and falling in love, of raising children and living happily ever after."

Derek looked at Ravine, and they both nodded. Isabel had already shown that to Derek in his sleep, and he recognized Nancy in the picture.

"Isabel Roberts was my grandmother's best friend," Mrs. Hill said. "Isabel wanted the fairy tale wedding, she was sure that dreams did come true, and she did believe in happily ever after. Everybody was always puzzled that these two very different girls were the best of friends. But they were inseparable."

She turned to another picture.

"They met when my grandmother was five years old. They would have known each other for about eleven years when Isabel died in the fire. Nancy was paralyzed with grief. Almost overnight, there was a change in her. She stopped challenging the rules and became less outgoing and more soft-spoken."

Turning the page, Mrs. Hill said, "Here is a picture of Isabel and my grandmother—Nana Nancy, I always called her. I think they were about fourteen when this one was taken."

Mrs. Hill paused as if she was searching her memory and then continued.

"This picture of my grandmother and her parents—my great grandparents—was taken not long after the fire. You can see the sadness in Nancy's eyes even though everyone else looks happy. After the fire, she visited Isabel's grave every day until the day she died herself. She even went to see Isabel on her wedding day. Sometimes she would go to the cemetery and spend hours telling Isabel what was going on at school, who was dating who, who hated who, who failed what, and all sorts of things. My grandmother believed she was Isabel's eyes and ears into this world."

Mrs. Hill paused again and asked Derek and Ravine if they wanted something to eat. Even though they had already eaten supper, Ravine nodded, thinking that would encourage the librarian to keep talking. Mrs. Hill disappeared into the kitchen and, when she came back, she had a tray of sandwiches and milk. Derek and Ravine helped themselves, and Mrs. Hill continued her story as she sipped a cup of tea.

"Nancy began to spend time with a boy named Jordan Burns. Jordan and Isabel had liked each other a lot, and everyone believed they would one day get married. Before Isabel's death, Nancy and Jordan hadn't really liked each other much. But the tragedy turned them into friends. Death changes people, they say, and it really changed my grandmother. She had always been a dreamer, and she did live out a dream. Only it wasn't her dream; it was Isabel's. She married Jordan Burns and lived the happily-ever-after dream of Isabel Roberts."

Ravine gawked at the librarian. Nancy married Isabel's true love! Did Isabel know this?

Mrs. Hill could see from their faces that more explanation was needed.

"Jordan was never able to forget Isabel," she said. "But neither could my grandmother. I guess the sorrow they shared brought them closer. I don't think they had the same kind of love as Jordan and Isabel, but I believe they became kindred spirits, finding comfort in each other and keeping Isabel alive through their memories. That, too, is a kind of love. Getting married was the only way they knew not to let go of Isabel."

Mrs. Hill seemed to be feeling unhappy as she continued.

"Nana Nancy and Jordan visited the grave together and apart. Even in death, Isabel was a big part of their lives. I never knew my Grandfather Jordan because he died before I was born. But my grandmother still visited the grave every day, and she often took me with her."

She hesitated briefly before continuing. "In fact, one day when she was very old, Nana Nancy went to visit Isabel's grave and never returned. She was found lying beside the grave, still clutching the forget-me-nots she had taken with her. I was told that she died peacefully."

The three chatted a little longer, but Mrs. Hill had already told them all she knew. Finally, Derek and Ravine said good-bye and thanked her for everything she had shared with them.

Ravine felt light-headed. Imagine loving someone that much, she thought. It seemed to Ravine that Isabel had two soul mates. Two people who would not let her die.

She glanced at Derek, wondering ...

Chapter Thirteen

When Ravine got home, she tore apart her room searching for the brown, stuffed bear, but it was nowhere to be found. She knew now that the bear had belonged to Sarah, but she wanted it back. She could not imagine how it had gotten to the bed in the convent.

She sat on her bed looking out the window toward 56 Water Street, replaying in her head everything Sister Catherine and Mrs. Hill had told them.

The lights across the street flickered.

On. Off. On. Off.

She could hear Isabel's faint voice calling to her, but she covered her ears and closed her eyes. Behind her eyelids, she could see the two sisters holding hands and smiling. And she could see Rachel smiling.

Ravine finally fell asleep and, when she did, a hand silently pulled her away from her own world into another dimension and time. A place and time when Sarah Roberts was alone.

Sarah stood in the middle of a garden picking forget-me-nots. They were her favorite flowers, especially the ones that grew wild. Isabel used to pick them for her.

"These flowers are called forget-me-nots," she'd say to Sarah. "I will never forget you, and when I am away from you, you shall never forget me. If you miss me when I am at school, all you have to do is pick some of these flowers and you will know I am thinking of you." Then she'd lift Sarah into the air and twirl her around, making her laugh.

The previous day had been sad for Sarah, even though the nuns had tried hard to make it happy. Since her first day with them, they had always tried to make her birthdays special. But this day was also the anniversary of the death of her family. How would she ever be able to enjoy another birthday?

They had baked her a chocolate cake and made her a new dress. They tried to make the simple party nice, and Sarah knew how much these women loved her. But she also knew she would never feel complete without her true family.

She was nine years old, and a third of her life had passed without her sister, her mother, and her father. Even though the nuns were her family now, she dreamed every night of the family that was gone, of the life that she would never have. She imagined that her parents and her sister had come back and were going to take her home. It was the only dream she had had during the last three years. It always caused her to wake in the morning with tears in her eyes and an overwhelming feeling of grief and sadness.

On this birthday, she had picked a bouquet of flowers for Mother Frances to decorate the supper table. She picked fresh flowers every Sunday as her small way of giving thanks to Mother Frances for taking care of her and loving her. Of course, she never said those words to the nun; she never said any words to anyone. There just wasn't anything to say anymore, and in the three years since the fire, she had not spoken another word. Sarah wasn't sure she even remembered how to speak. The nuns had never told her that she often cried out for her sister in her sleep.

The last word she ever spoke while awake was on the night of the fire, when she cried out in fear. The one word was "Isabel." But her sister never came for her. She learned later that Isabel couldn't come because the fire had consumed her.

Ravine tossed in her sleep and, just when she felt herself being pulled away from the garden of flowers, she was swept further into the future of Sarah's life, just a few months after her ninth birthday.

It was early autumn, and Mother Frances sat beside Sarah's bed, patting the girl's forehead with a cold, damp cloth. Sarah was racked with fever, but her little body shook from a chill. She had been lying like this for too many days, and Mother Frances's tears fell as she tended the patient. She knew that soon she would not see Sarah's twinkling green eyes or her sad smile again. She loved Sarah like a daughter and quietly lamented that God was taking Sarah away from her so soon.

Of course she knew why God was doing this. Sarah could no longer live in a world that had robbed her of her sister and parents. But that didn't lessen Mother Frances's pain, and she let the tears flow freely down her face.

Mother Frances sat with Sarah through that night and the next night, until the little body passed gently away.

It was late, and Derek stood looking through his window, watching the house across the street. He could see the lights flickering on and off. A hundred years was a long time to look for someone. The old weeping willow waved and swayed, even though the air was calm.

A sudden gust of wind rushed through his open window and, from behind him, a cold hand touched his shoulder. He turned quickly to find Isabel standing behind him in her long, grey dress, holding a bouquet of dying flowers. Her eyes were dull now, no longer a brilliant green, and she seemed to be fading in and out of focus.

She floated toward him. "If I do not find her soon, I will be here forever. Please find her. I want to go home, but my time is running out." The colour of her eyes faded a bit more, and she was gone before he could tell her where Sarah was.

Derek didn't move. Her words repeated themselves in his mind: "Please find her ... I want to go home ... my time is running out."

He walked slowly to his bed, hearing the words echo in his head. He realized if they couldn't get Isabel to Sarah's grave and show her that Sarah had already crossed over to the light, that she had already gone home, Isabel might be a ghost forever. He thought about her eyes, and instinctively he understood her eyes were the key. Once all the colour had faded from them, she would be a ghost forever.

He sat on his bed hoping he and Ravine had enough time to send Isabel home. He looked at the clock: almost midnight. He sat motionless for a couple of minutes and then walked to his door, quietly opening it. He knew what he had to do.

He looked down the hallway. The lights were off and the door to his mother's room was closed; so was his sister's. He listened for a few minutes, but all was quiet.

Carefully watching where he stepped, he tiptoed past their rooms and made his way quietly down the stairs. The house was dark, and he held his arm in front of him so he wouldn't bump into anything.

He opened the front door, stepped outside, and closed the door silently behind him, then ran down the driveway without looking back.

Halfway to Ravine's house, he stopped running. His heart was beating fast, not because he was tired from running, but because he had actually snuck out of the house. The feeling of freedom was overwhelming as he walked to the front of Ravine's house and approached her bedroom window.

Tap! Tap! Tap! Ravine opened her eyes as she heard it again. *Tap! Tap! Tap!* She got out of bed and opened her curtains just as another pebble came flying toward the window. She looked down and saw Derek throwing stones.

"What are you doing?" she whispered.

"Get dressed and meet me at fifty-six," he replied. Then, without saying another word, he turned and headed straight toward Isabel's ghostly castle.

Ravine dressed quickly and opened her bedroom door a couple of inches. She looked up and down the hall and, when she was certain her parents were sleeping, she crept down the stairs and out the front door.

She saw Derek standing on the front porch of Isabel's house, and she ran across the street to meet him.

"What's this all about?" Ravine asked.

"We have to find Isabel tonight and tell her where Sarah is buried. We don't have much time left."

"What do you mean, we don't have much time left?" she asked, opening the door. It was dark. It was darker than dark.

"Isabel came to see me tonight, and she told me that if we don't find Sarah soon, she will be a ghost forever."

They walked into the house, and Ravine yelled, "Isabel! Isabel! We know where Sarah is!"

They stood waiting and looking, but Isabel didn't appear.

"Isabel," Derek yelled, "we know where Sarah is!"

They waited, and suddenly they each felt a cold hand on their shoulders.

Isabel stood behind them, and her eyes were duller than when Derek had seen them earlier. He could see they didn't have much time.

"Sarah died when she was nine years old and was buried in the cemetery behind the convent. That's why you could never find her," Derek said.

"Take me, please; take me now!" Isabel said.

Without their bikes, it took them much longer to get to the convent. Isabel floated along in front of them, feverishly swaying back and forth as she urged them to hurry.

"How are we going to get in?" Derek asked when they finally reached the gates. Isabel floated around as her eyes became duller and duller.

"I do not have much time," she said, frantically. Then she floated over the gates and looked behind her, waiting for Derek and Ravine to follow. But they just stood there.

"If you want it badly, you have to go get it," Isabel said, desperately.

"What does she mean?" Derek asked Ravine.

"I think she wants us to figure out how to get in. Look, that tree is pretty close to the wall. I think if we climb it, we can jump to the top of the wall," Ravine said.

He shook his head. "That's a pretty big jump down on the other side. And then how do we get back out?" After looking around quickly, he added, "Why don't we just climb the iron gate? We should be able to get over it from either side without having to kill ourselves with a big jump."

Ravine looked at Isabel. Time was running out.

"Okay," she said. "Let's try it."

Even though the gate was large and imposing, it was surprisingly easy to climb, and in just a few minutes, they were over it and racing past the garden to the little graveyard, with Isabel floating along beside them. They stopped at the grave of Sarah Roberts.

Isabel bent down. "Oh, Sarah, my dear sister. Sarah."

Ravine and Derek watched as Isabel hovered over her sister's grave, reading the inscription.

"The last word she ever spoke was your name. The night the house burned down," Ravine offered. "She never spoke another word after that night."

"The nuns took care of her until she died of pneumonia when she was nine years old," Derek said, looking at Isabel's eyes.

They were gradually getting brighter and greener.

Isabel began to float higher above the two children, and, when they looked up, they saw a white glow in the sky. It was as if there was a sudden opening into another place, different from the world in which they lived, and a bright light was shining through the opening.

"Isabel!" Sarah cried.

In the warmth of the soft glow, Sarah stood above them, reaching out her arms and calling to her long-lost sister.

Isabel floated higher and higher, and the greyness that once surrounded her became pure white.

Ravine smiled.

As Derek and Ravine watched the girls embrace, Sarah held out a bouquet of forget-me-nots to her sister.

"Never forget me, and I'll never forget you," Sarah said, handing Isabel the flowers. "Remember?"

"Yes, I remember," said Isabel.

Isabel looked down at the two children who had helped bring her home. She smiled, and they could see the gratitude in her bright green eyes. Then, with a flash of light, she and Sarah were gone.

Ravine bent down, picking up the flowers and whispering, "Never forget me, and I'll never forget you."

Derek put his arms around Ravine, and they silently hugged, grateful they had been able to help. Grateful for each other.

Chapter Fourteen

Ravine stretched out her arms as the sun peeked through her bedroom curtains. She yawned, and her fingers touched something soft. She opened her eyes and found Sarah's brown teddy bear beside her. Ravine hugged the bear tightly and rolled over. As she fell back to sleep, a familiar voice whispered in her ear, "I love you." Rachel bent down to give Ravine a hug, and then she was gone. But her warmth stayed with Ravine.

Derek opened his eyes and lay still, thinking about Isabel. He would miss her, but he was glad she was finally where she was supposed to be.

He got out of bed and opened the curtains. The sun was particularly bright this morning. He looked across the road to 56 Water Street and smiled. The house was gone. The weeping willow was gone. All that was left was an empty lot filled with forget-me-nots growing wild in the grass. Isabel was home.

Derek sat down at his desk, took out a pencil, a piece of paper, and some charcoal and began to draw. He sat at his desk all morning, drawing the house that had been forgotten so long ago by the people on Water Street. He would never forget the girl with the long, dark hair and cat-like eyes.

He'd never forget. And now he'd bring back a piece of history.

When he finished his picture, he wrote at the top of the page: "56 Water Street." He wrote a short essay about Isabel and Sarah Roberts and then he placed it and the drawing in a brown envelope and addressed it to "The Mike Markle Contest."

As Derek walked down the stairs, he could hear Danielle and his mom arguing. He walked into the kitchen and gave Danielle a hug.

"I love you, Danielle," he said. "Never forget that." Then he grabbed an apple and walked out the back door, leaving his mother and sister stunned.

He bit into his apple and walked across the street to where Ravine was sitting, and he sat down beside her.

"The house is gone," she said sadly. She was picking the wildflowers.

"I know," he said.

"I knew it would be gone; it's just that it feels so empty."

Ravine was quiet and a tear escaped and rolled down her cheek. "Do you think she'll remember us?" she asked.

Derek picked a flower and gave it to her.

"She'll never forget," he said smiling.

1329480

Made in the USA